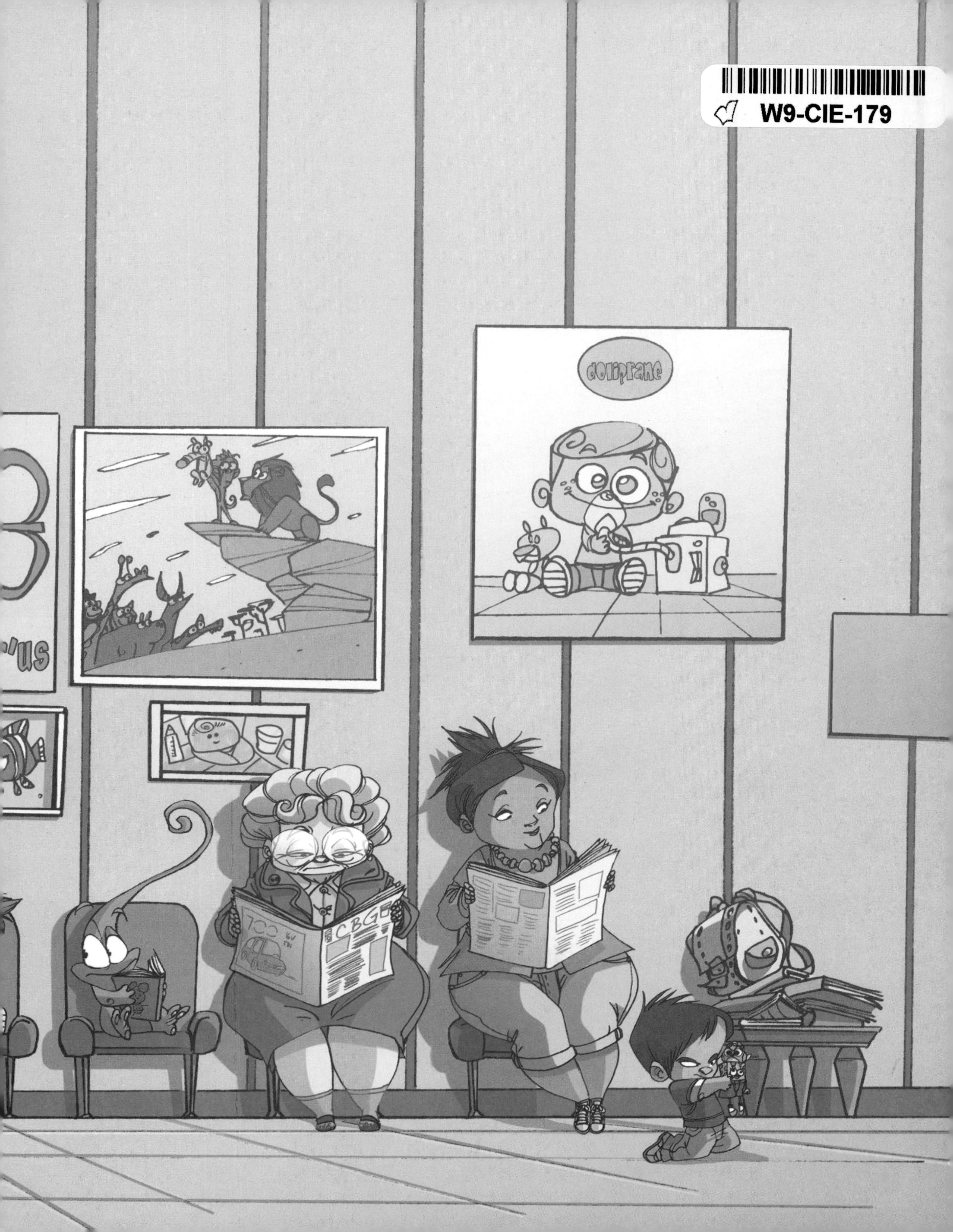
doliprane
CBG

Ernest & Rebecca

"My Best Friend is a Germ"

Guillaume Bianco — Writer
Antonello Dalena — Artist
Cecilia Giumento — Colorist

PAPERCUTZ™
New York

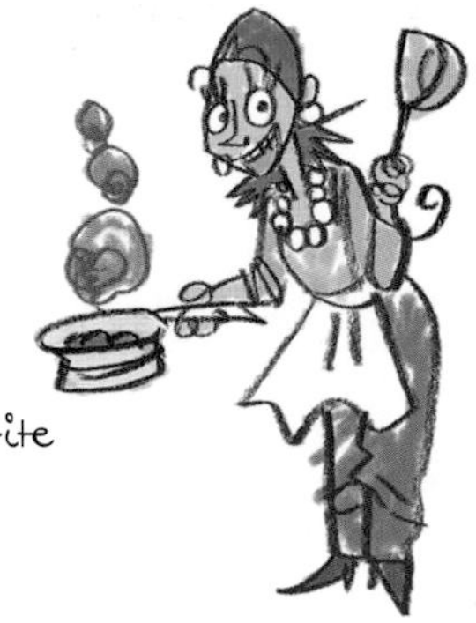

Mommy

She's the most beautiful mommy of all! She's not at home a lot because of her job, but she always finds time to cook my favorite food for me: "steak and fries with ketchup and mayonnaise!"

Daddy

He's an artist. A painter... like Picasso, but better! We have lots of fun together when mommy's at work... He's the funniest daddy of all!

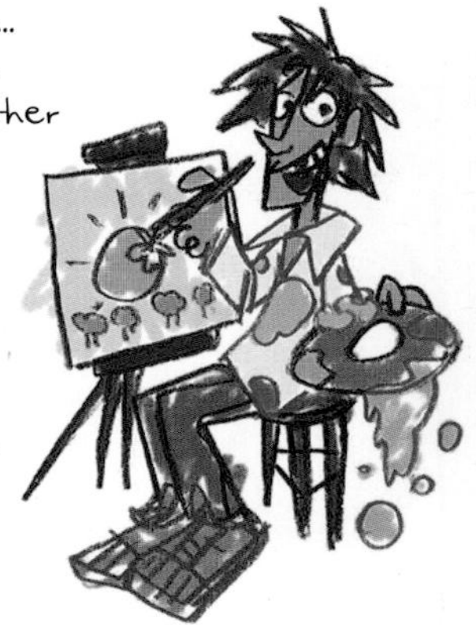

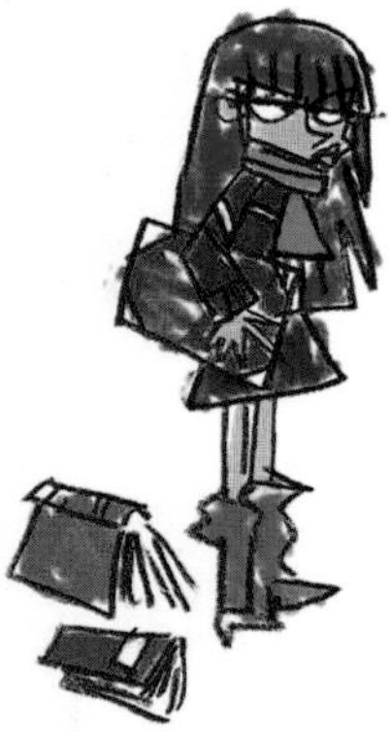

Coralie

She's my big sister. I adore her, even if, ever since she's been her rebellious stage, she stays in her room all the time.

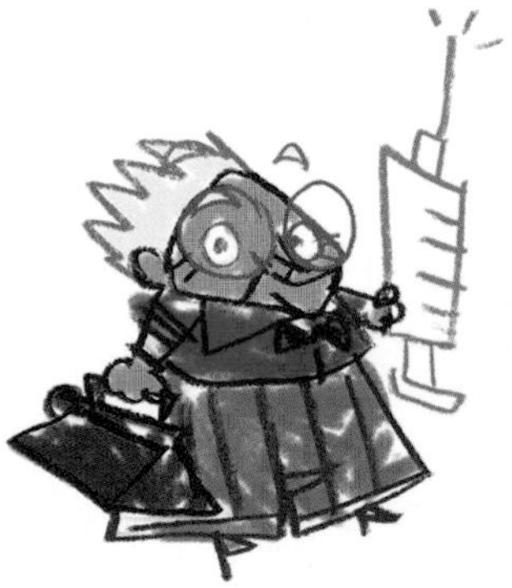

Dr. Fakbert

He's awful as a doctor. He often comes to the house to take care of me... You've got to wonder why I'm always sick!

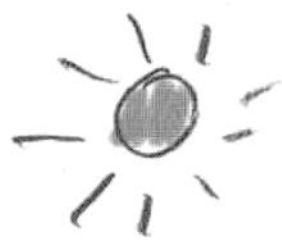

Ernest

He's a microbe... and he's my best friend! I caught him one day while on a frog hunt. Since then, we're always together... He's super smart and really strong: he can change into anything!

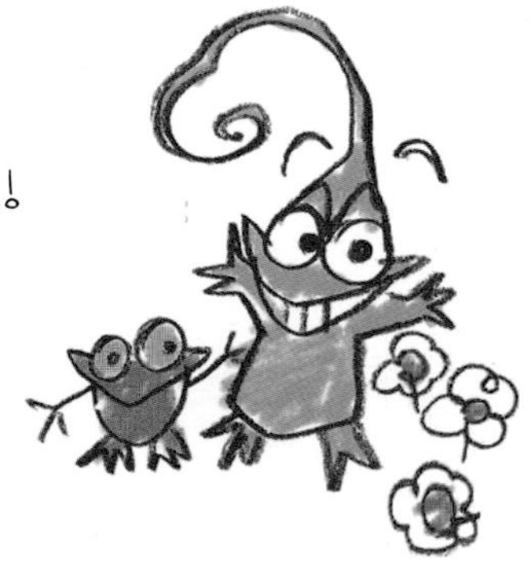

And me: Rebecca

I'm not very big... It's 'cause I hate soup! I'd rather eat ketchup and chase frogs with Ernest in the rain!

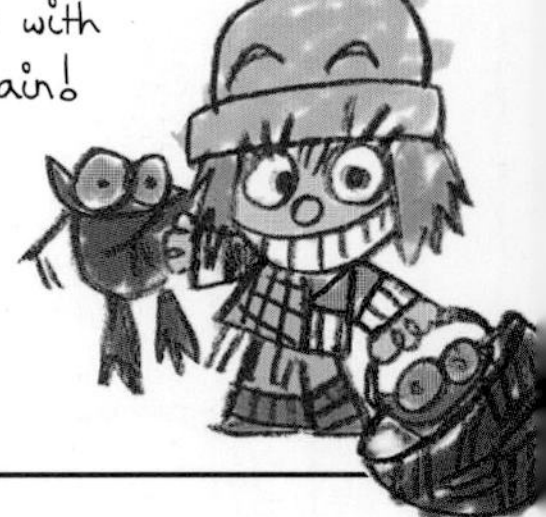

Ernest & Rebecca™
#1 "My Best Friend is a Germ"

Guillaume Bianco – Writer
Antonello Dalena – Artist
Cecilia Giumento – Colorist
Jean-Luc Deglin – Original Design
Joe Johnson – Translation
Janice Chiang – Lettering
Production – Chris Nelson, Nelson Design Group, LLC
Associate Editor – Michael Petranek
Jim Salicrup
Editor-in-Chief

ISBN: 978-1-59707-286-1

Printed in China
November 2011 by PWGS
Block 623 Aljunied Road #07-03B
Aljunied Industrial Complex 389835

Distributed by Macmillan.
First Papercutz Printing

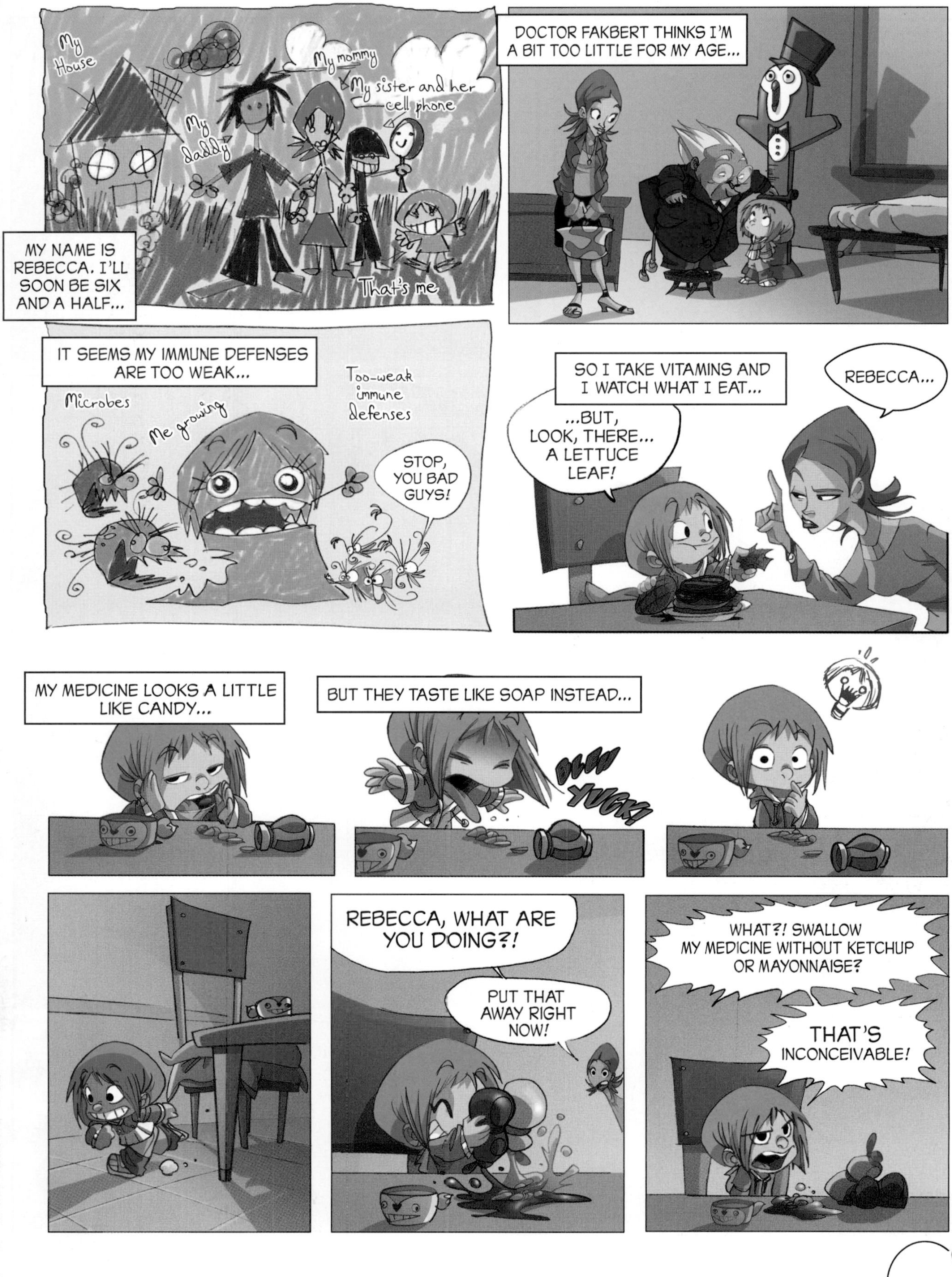
MY NAME IS REBECCA. I'LL SOON BE SIX AND A HALF...
My House
My mommy
My sister and her cell phone
My daddy
That's me
DOCTOR FAKBERT THINKS I'M A BIT TOO LITTLE FOR MY AGE...
IT SEEMS MY IMMUNE DEFENSES ARE TOO WEAK...
Microbes
Me growing
Too-weak immune defenses
STOP, YOU BAD GUYS!
SO I TAKE VITAMINS AND I WATCH WHAT I EAT...
...BUT, LOOK, THERE... A LETTUCE LEAF!
REBECCA...
MY MEDICINE LOOKS A LITTLE LIKE CANDY...
BUT THEY TASTE LIKE SOAP INSTEAD...
BLEH
YUCK!
REBECCA, WHAT ARE YOU DOING?!
PUT THAT AWAY RIGHT NOW!
WHAT?! SWALLOW MY MEDICINE WITHOUT KETCHUP OR MAYONNAISE?
THAT'S INCONCEIVABLE!

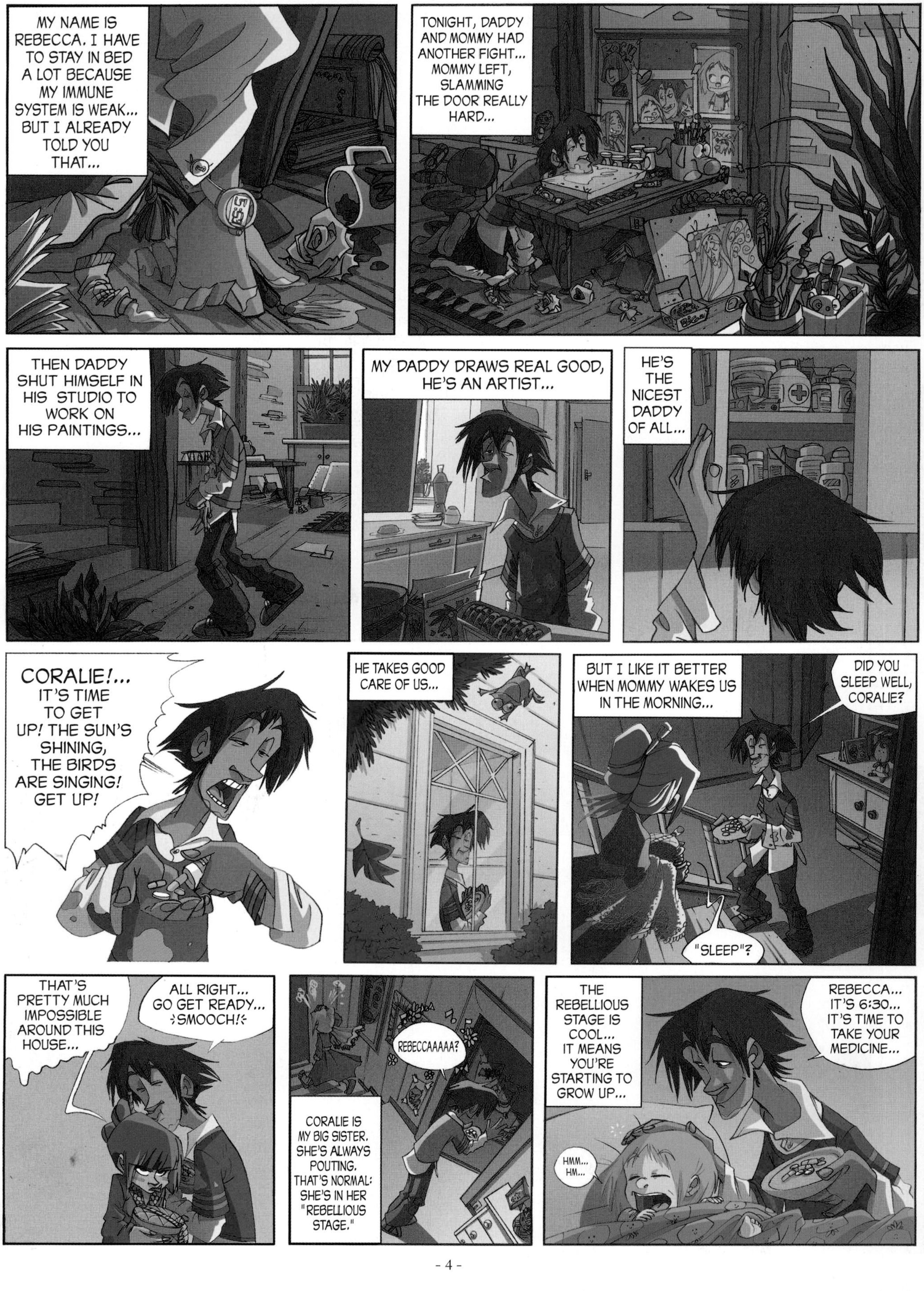
MY NAME IS REBECCA. I HAVE TO STAY IN BED A LOT BECAUSE MY IMMUNE SYSTEM IS WEAK... BUT I ALREADY TOLD YOU THAT...
TONIGHT, DADDY AND MOMMY HAD ANOTHER FIGHT... MOMMY LEFT, SLAMMING THE DOOR REALLY HARD...
THEN DADDY SHUT HIMSELF IN HIS STUDIO TO WORK ON HIS PAINTINGS...
MY DADDY DRAWS REAL GOOD, HE'S AN ARTIST...
HE'S THE NICEST DADDY OF ALL...
CORALIE!... IT'S TIME TO GET UP! THE SUN'S SHINING, THE BIRDS ARE SINGING! GET UP!
HE TAKES GOOD CARE OF US...
BUT I LIKE IT BETTER WHEN MOMMY WAKES US IN THE MORNING...
DID YOU SLEEP WELL, CORALIE?
"SLEEP"?
THAT'S PRETTY MUCH IMPOSSIBLE AROUND THIS HOUSE...
ALL RIGHT... GO GET READY... SMOOCH!
REBECCAAAAA?
CORALIE IS MY BIG SISTER. SHE'S ALWAYS POUTING. THAT'S NORMAL: SHE'S IN HER "REBELLIOUS STAGE."
THE REBELLIOUS STAGE IS COOL... IT MEANS YOU'RE STARTING TO GROW UP...
REBECCA... IT'S 6:30... IT'S TIME TO TAKE YOUR MEDICINE...
HMM... HM...

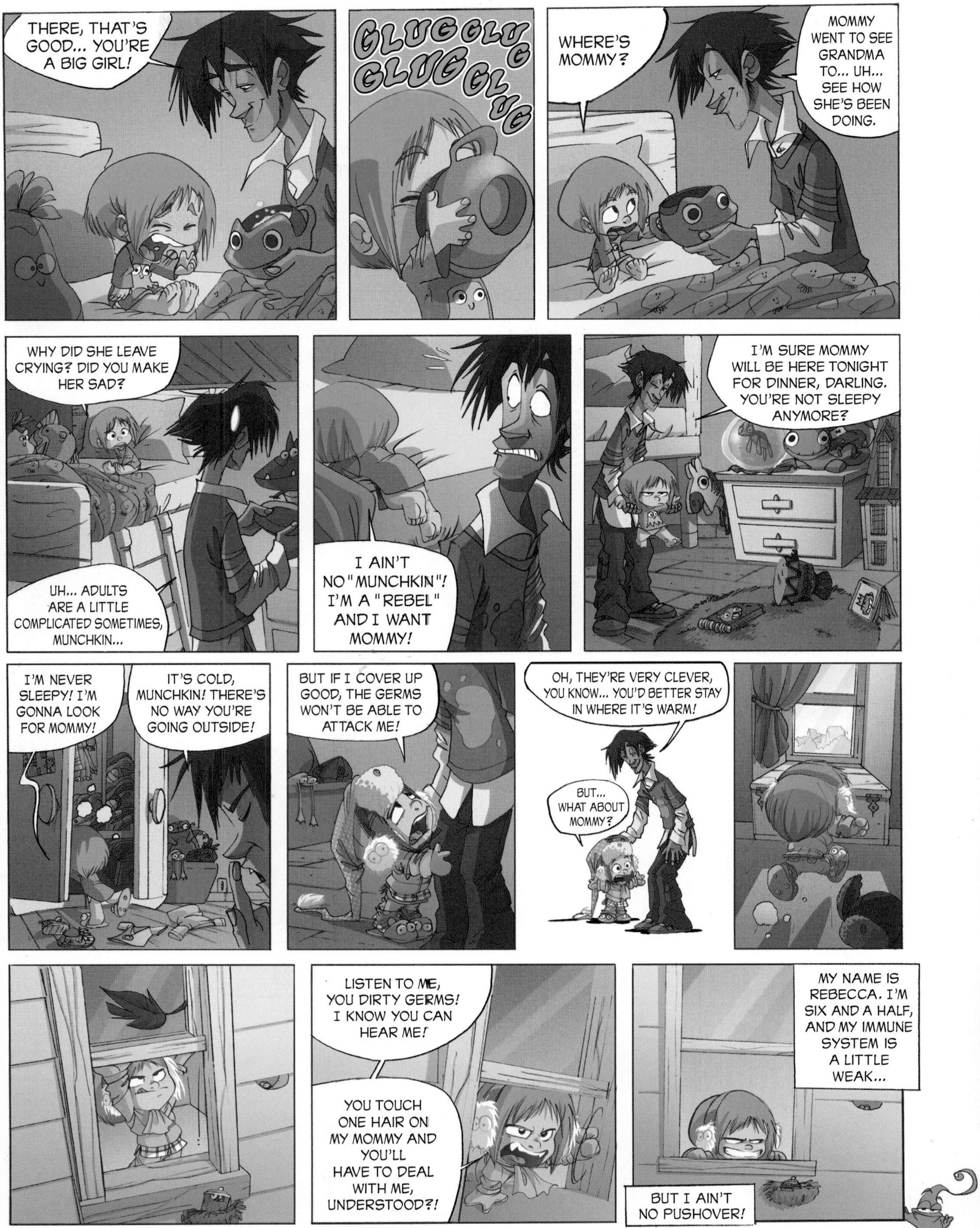

THERE, THAT'S GOOD... YOU'RE A BIG GIRL!
GLUG GLUG GLUG GLUG
WHERE'S MOMMY?
MOMMY WENT TO SEE GRANDMA TO... UH... SEE HOW SHE'S BEEN DOING.
WHY DID SHE LEAVE CRYING? DID YOU MAKE HER SAD?
UH... ADULTS ARE A LITTLE COMPLICATED SOMETIMES, MUNCHKIN...
I AIN'T NO "MUNCHKIN"! I'M A "REBEL" AND I WANT MOMMY!
I'M SURE MOMMY WILL BE HERE TONIGHT FOR DINNER, DARLING. YOU'RE NOT SLEEPY ANYMORE?
I'M NEVER SLEEPY! I'M GONNA LOOK FOR MOMMY!
IT'S COLD, MUNCHKIN! THERE'S NO WAY YOU'RE GOING OUTSIDE!
BUT IF I COVER UP GOOD, THE GERMS WON'T BE ABLE TO ATTACK ME!
OH, THEY'RE VERY CLEVER, YOU KNOW... YOU'D BETTER STAY IN WHERE IT'S WARM!
BUT... WHAT ABOUT MOMMY?
LISTEN TO ME, YOU DIRTY GERMS! I KNOW YOU CAN HEAR ME!
YOU TOUCH ONE HAIR ON MY MOMMY AND YOU'LL HAVE TO DEAL WITH ME, UNDERSTOOD?!
MY NAME IS REBECCA. I'M SIX AND A HALF, AND MY IMMUNE SYSTEM IS A LITTLE WEAK...
BUT I AIN'T NO PUSHOVER!

THE OTHER DAY, MOMMY AND ME WENT BACK TO SEE DR. FAKBERT...

HELLO, DOCTOR.

HELLO! HAVE A SEAT...

HE LOOKED AT MY DRAWINGS FOR A LONG TIME...

HMMM.. YES... I SEE!

HE TOLD ME TO NOT WORRY ABOUT BEING LITTLE, THAT IT WOULD WORK ITSELF OUT.*

My House

Me

THEN HE ASKED ME A FUNNY QUESTION...

Daddy

Mommy

SAY, REBECCA--

"REBECCA" HA HA!

DO YOU PREFER...

...YOUR DADDY...

...OR YOUR MOMMY?...

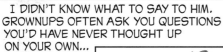

I DIDN'T KNOW WHAT TO SAY TO HIM. GROWNUPS OFTEN ASK YOU QUESTIONS YOU'D HAVE NEVER THOUGHT UP ON YOUR OWN...

AND BESIDES... A DADDY AND A MOMMY ARE LIKE KETCHUP AND MAYONNAISE...

THEY'RE BETTER TOGETHER.

*OBVIOUSLY, REBECCA ENJOYS READING "THE SMURFS"— ALSO AVAILABLE FROM PAPERCUTZ!

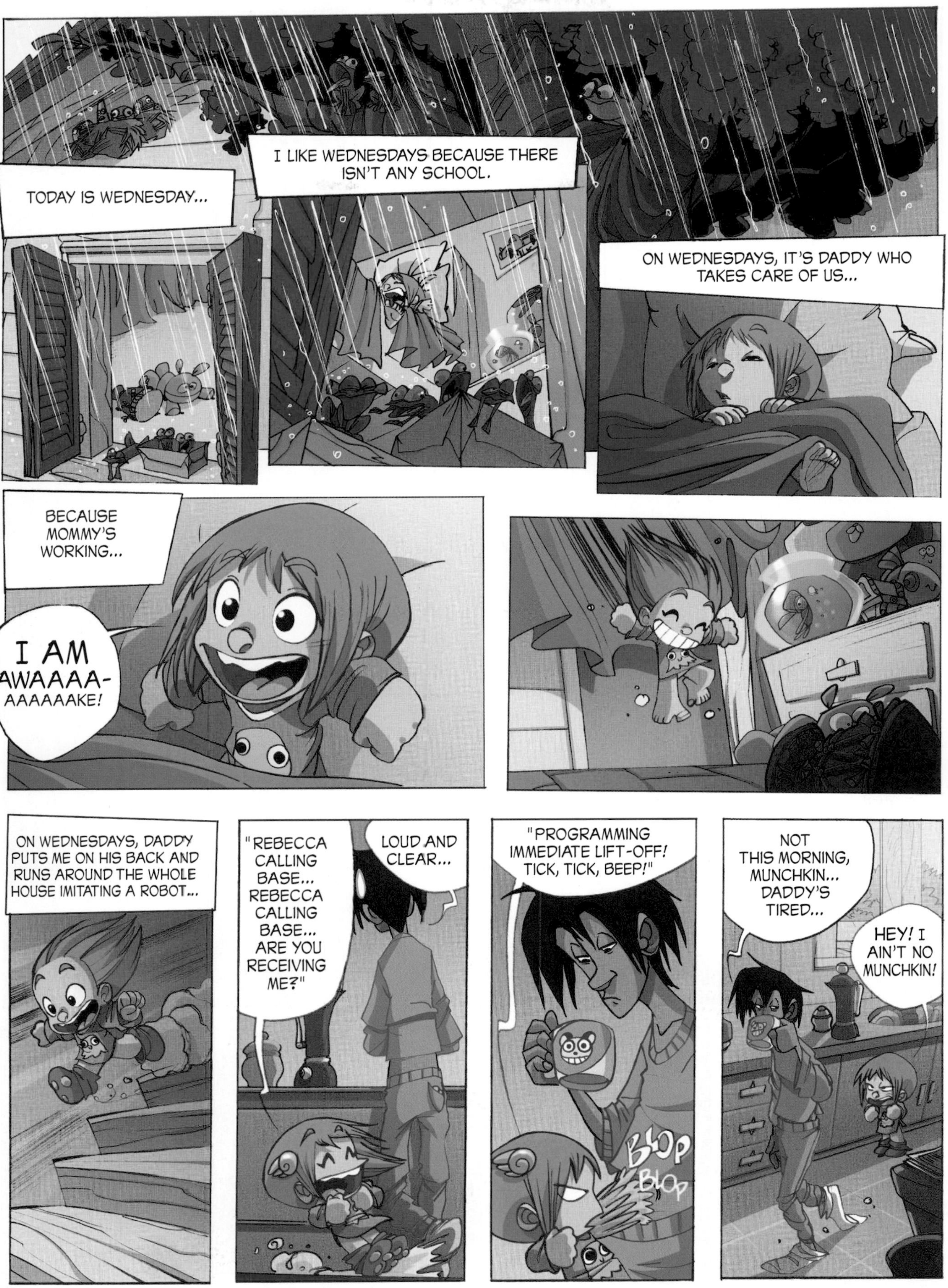
TODAY IS WEDNESDAY...
I LIKE WEDNESDAYS BECAUSE THERE ISN'T ANY SCHOOL.
ON WEDNESDAYS, IT'S DADDY WHO TAKES CARE OF US...
BECAUSE MOMMY'S WORKING...
I AM AWAAAA-AAAAAAKE!
ON WEDNESDAYS, DADDY PUTS ME ON HIS BACK AND RUNS AROUND THE WHOLE HOUSE IMITATING A ROBOT...
"REBECCA CALLING BASE... REBECCA CALLING BASE... ARE YOU RECEIVING ME?"
LOUD AND CLEAR...
"PROGRAMMING IMMEDIATE LIFT-OFF! TICK, TICK, BEEP!"
BLOP
BLOP
NOT THIS MORNING, MUNCHKIN... DADDY'S TIRED...
HEY! I AIN'T NO MUNCHKIN!

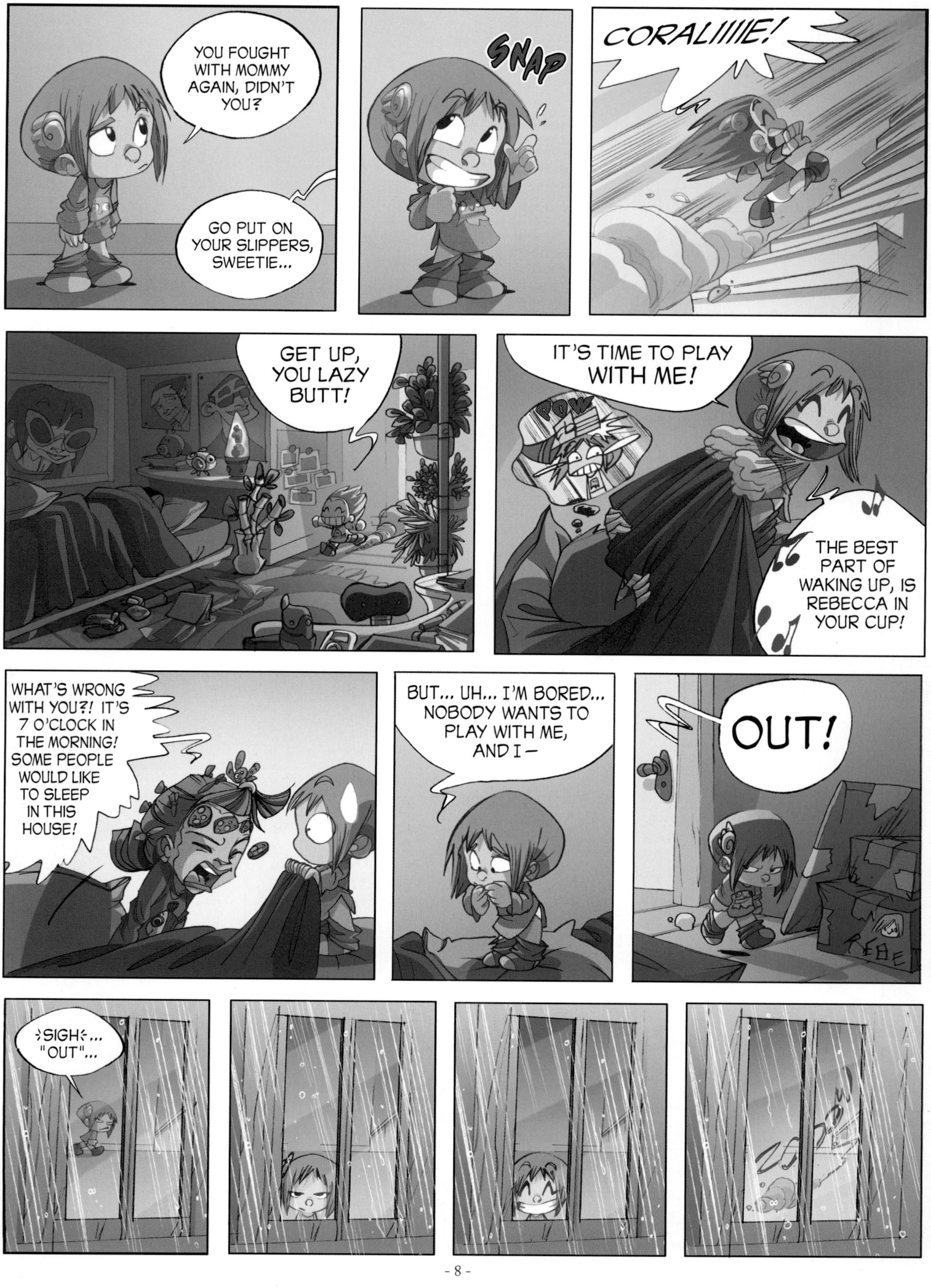
YOU FOUGHT WITH MOMMY AGAIN, DIDN'T YOU?
GO PUT ON YOUR SLIPPERS, SWEETIE...
SNAP
CORALIIIIE!
GET UP, YOU LAZY BUTT!
IT'S TIME TO PLAY WITH ME!
POW
THE BEST PART OF WAKING UP, IS REBECCA IN YOUR CUP!
WHAT'S WRONG WITH YOU?! IT'S 7 O'CLOCK IN THE MORNING! SOME PEOPLE WOULD LIKE TO SLEEP IN THIS HOUSE!
BUT... UH... I'M BORED... NOBODY WANTS TO PLAY WITH ME, AND I—
OUT!
SIGH... "OUT"...

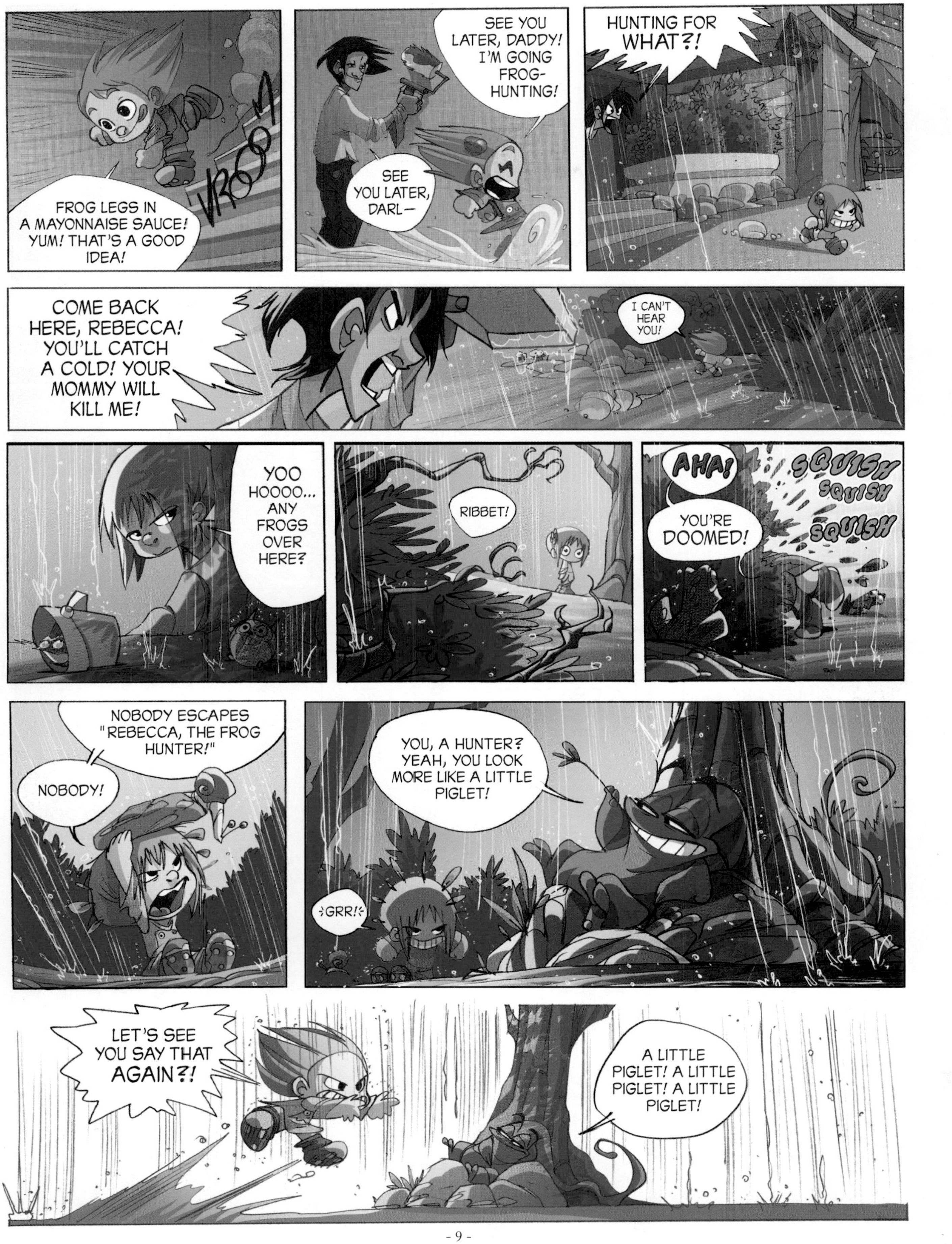
FROG LEGS IN A MAYONNAISE SAUCE! YUM! THAT'S A GOOD IDEA!
VROOOM
SEE YOU LATER, DADDY! I'M GOING FROG-HUNTING!
SEE YOU LATER, DARL—
HUNTING FOR WHAT?!
COME BACK HERE, REBECCA! YOU'LL CATCH A COLD! YOUR MOMMY WILL KILL ME!
I CAN'T HEAR YOU!
YOO HOOOO... ANY FROGS OVER HERE?
RIBBET!
AHA!
YOU'RE DOOMED!
SQUISH
SQUISH
SQUISH
NOBODY ESCAPES "REBECCA, THE FROG HUNTER!"
NOBODY!
YOU, A HUNTER? YEAH, YOU LOOK MORE LIKE A LITTLE PIGLET!
GRR!
LET'S SEE YOU SAY THAT AGAIN?!
A LITTLE PIGLET! A LITTLE PIGLET! A LITTLE PIGLET!

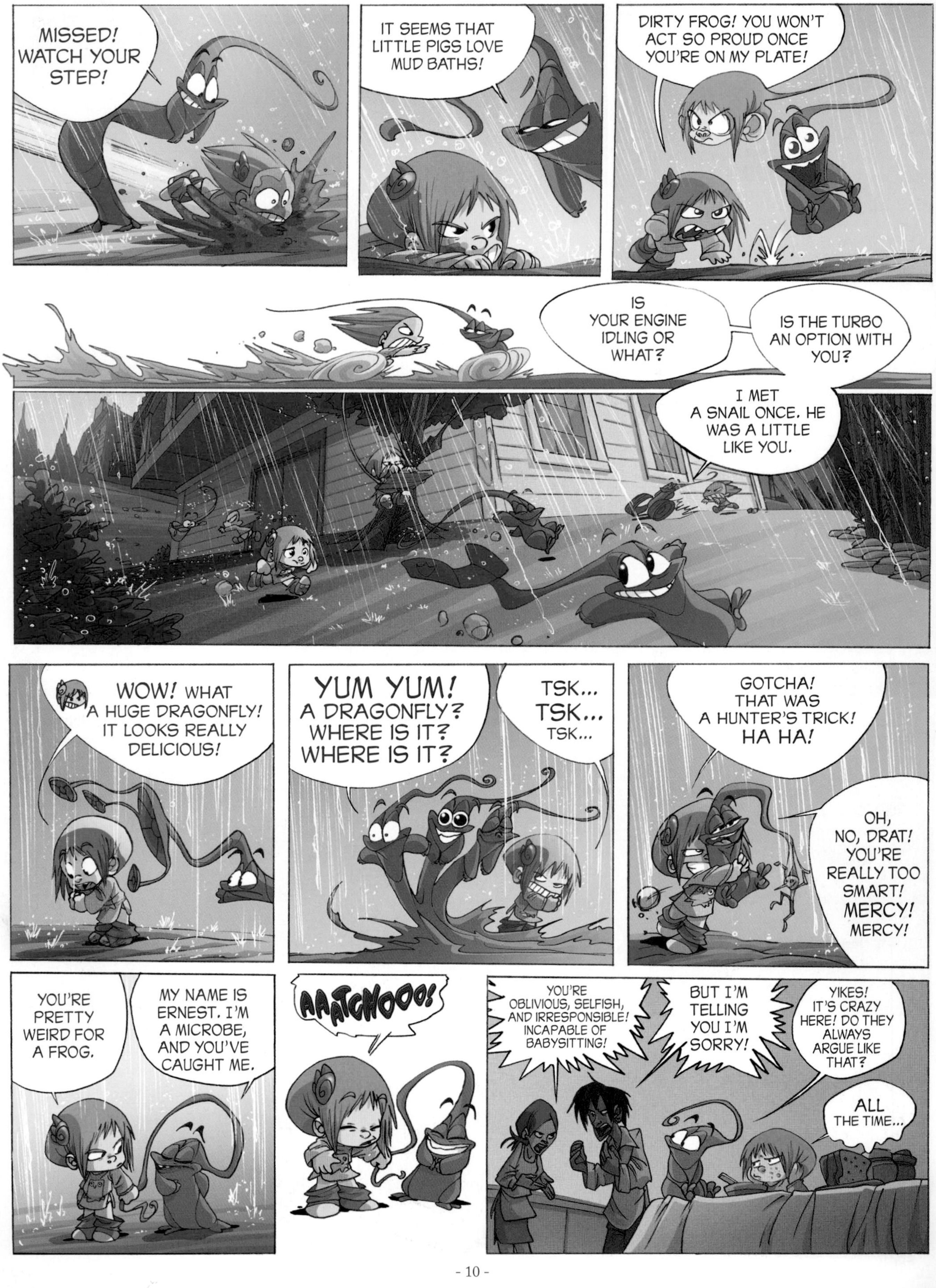
MISSED! WATCH YOUR STEP!
IT SEEMS THAT LITTLE PIGS LOVE MUD BATHS!
DIRTY FROG! YOU WON'T ACT SO PROUD ONCE YOU'RE ON MY PLATE!
IS YOUR ENGINE IDLING OR WHAT?
IS THE TURBO AN OPTION WITH YOU?
I MET A SNAIL ONCE. HE WAS A LITTLE LIKE YOU.
WOW! WHAT A HUGE DRAGONFLY! IT LOOKS REALLY DELICIOUS!
YUM YUM! A DRAGONFLY? WHERE IS IT? WHERE IS IT?
TSK... TSK... TSK...
GOTCHA! THAT WAS A HUNTER'S TRICK! HA HA!
OH, NO, DRAT! YOU'RE REALLY TOO SMART! MERCY! MERCY!
YOU'RE PRETTY WEIRD FOR A FROG.
MY NAME IS ERNEST. I'M A MICROBE, AND YOU'VE CAUGHT ME.
AAATCHOOO!
YOU'RE OBLIVIOUS, SELFISH, AND IRRESPONSIBLE! INCAPABLE OF BABYSITTING!
BUT I'M TELLING YOU I'M SORRY!
YIKES! IT'S CRAZY HERE! DO THEY ALWAYS ARGUE LIKE THAT?
ALL THE TIME...

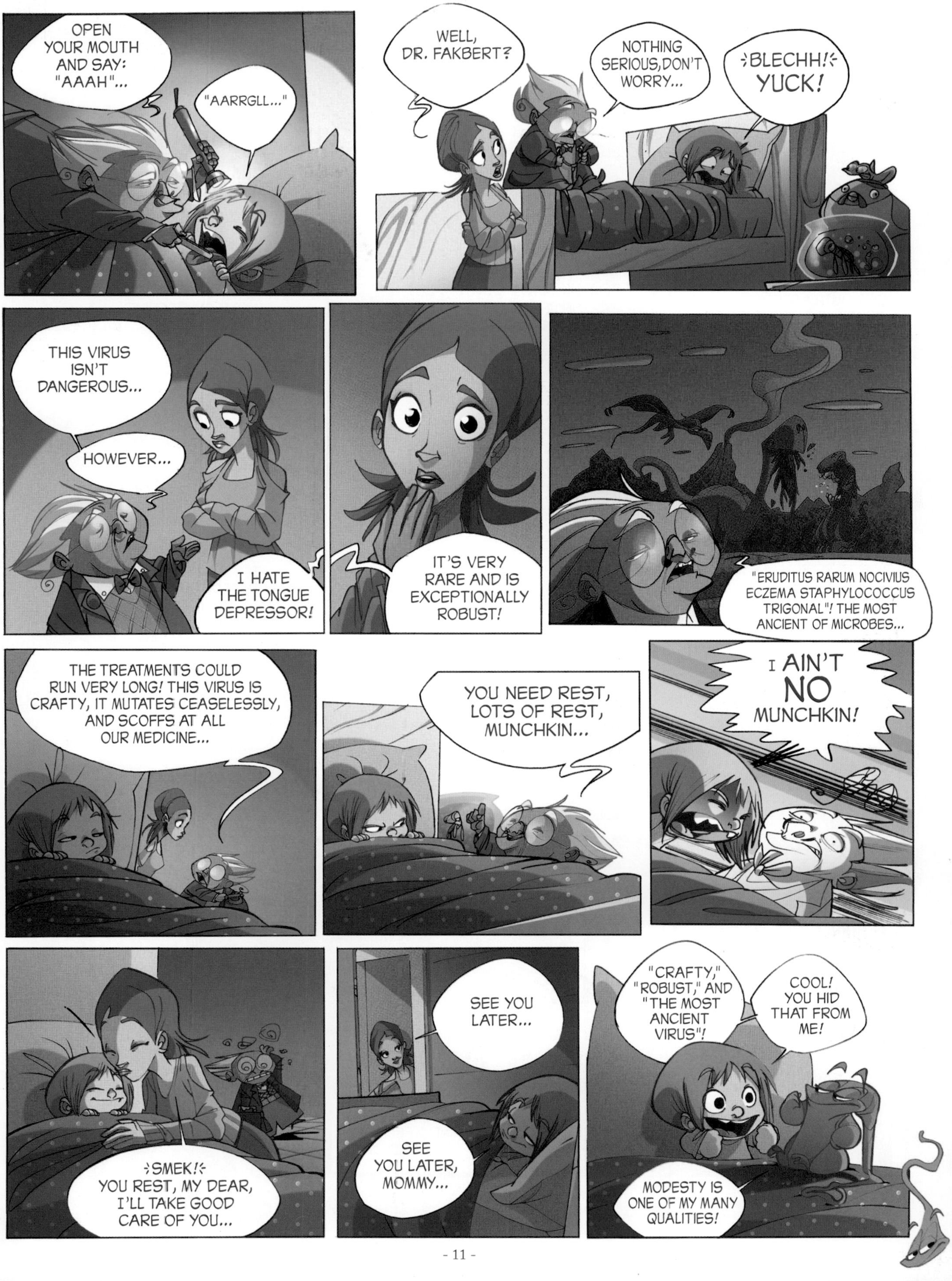
OPEN YOUR MOUTH AND SAY: "AAAH"...
"AARRGLL..."
WELL, DR. FAKBERT?
NOTHING SERIOUS, DON'T WORRY...
BLECHH! YUCK!
THIS VIRUS ISN'T DANGEROUS...
HOWEVER...
I HATE THE TONGUE DEPRESSOR!
IT'S VERY RARE AND IS EXCEPTIONALLY ROBUST!
"ERUDITUS RARUM NOCIVIUS ECZEMA STAPHYLOCOCCUS TRIGONAL"! THE MOST ANCIENT OF MICROBES...
THE TREATMENTS COULD RUN VERY LONG! THIS VIRUS IS CRAFTY, IT MUTATES CEASELESSLY, AND SCOFFS AT ALL OUR MEDICINE...
YOU NEED REST, LOTS OF REST, MUNCHKIN...
I AIN'T NO MUNCHKIN!
SMEK! YOU REST, MY DEAR, I'LL TAKE GOOD CARE OF YOU...
SEE YOU LATER...
SEE YOU LATER, MOMMY...
"CRAFTY," "ROBUST," AND "THE MOST ANCIENT VIRUS"!
COOL! YOU HID THAT FROM ME!
MODESTY IS ONE OF MY MANY QUALITIES!

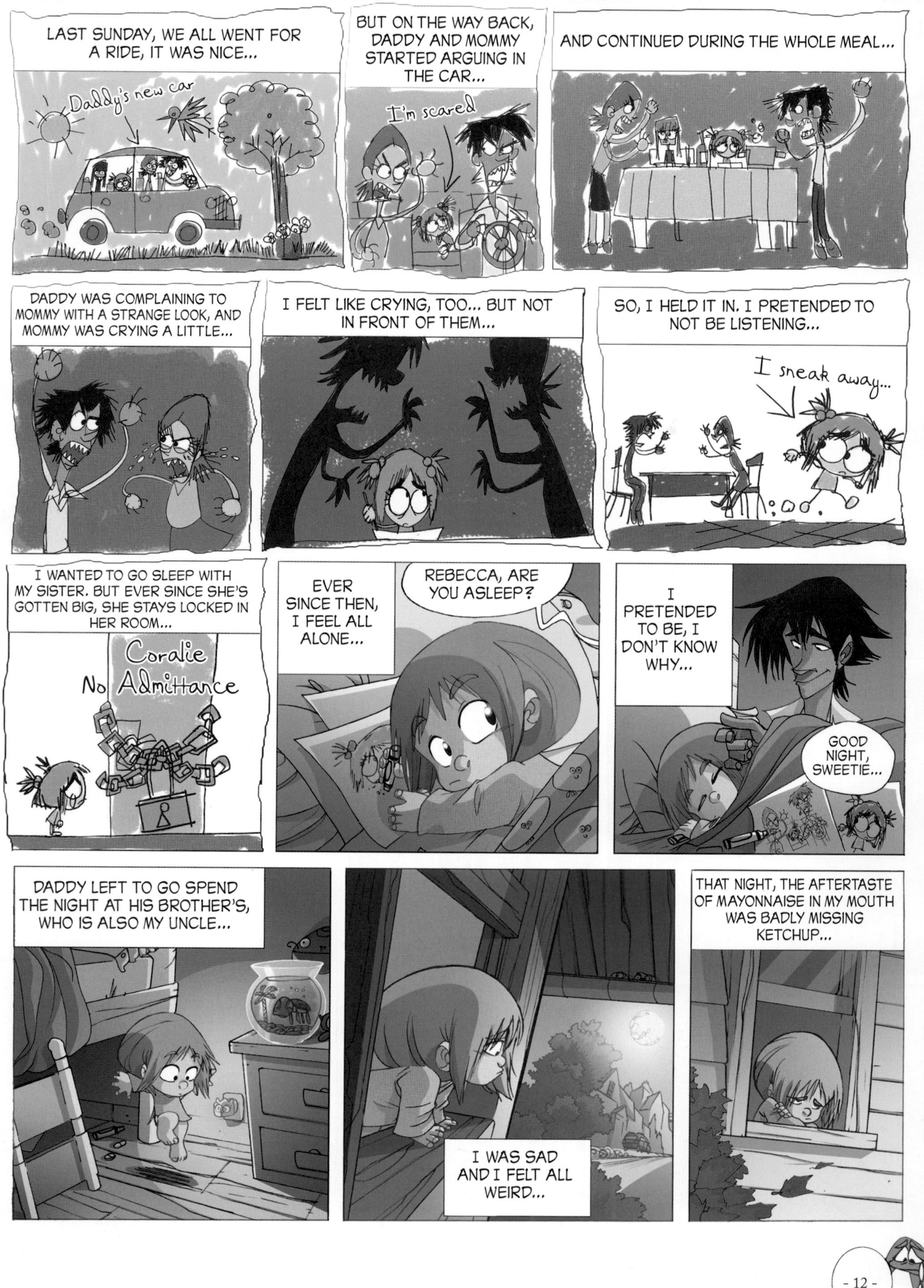
LAST SUNDAY, WE ALL WENT FOR A RIDE, IT WAS NICE...
Daddy's new car
BUT ON THE WAY BACK, DADDY AND MOMMY STARTED ARGUING IN THE CAR...
I'm scared
AND CONTINUED DURING THE WHOLE MEAL...
DADDY WAS COMPLAINING TO MOMMY WITH A STRANGE LOOK, AND MOMMY WAS CRYING A LITTLE...
I FELT LIKE CRYING, TOO... BUT NOT IN FRONT OF THEM...
SO, I HELD IT IN. I PRETENDED TO NOT BE LISTENING...
I sneak away...
I WANTED TO GO SLEEP WITH MY SISTER. BUT EVER SINCE SHE'S GOTTEN BIG, SHE STAYS LOCKED IN HER ROOM...
Coralie
No Admittance
EVER SINCE THEN, I FEEL ALL ALONE...
REBECCA, ARE YOU ASLEEP?
I PRETENDED TO BE, I DON'T KNOW WHY...
GOOD NIGHT, SWEETIE...
DADDY LEFT TO GO SPEND THE NIGHT AT HIS BROTHER'S, WHO IS ALSO MY UNCLE...
I WAS SAD AND I FELT ALL WEIRD...
THAT NIGHT, THE AFTERTASTE OF MAYONNAISE IN MY MOUTH WAS BADLY MISSING KETCHUP...

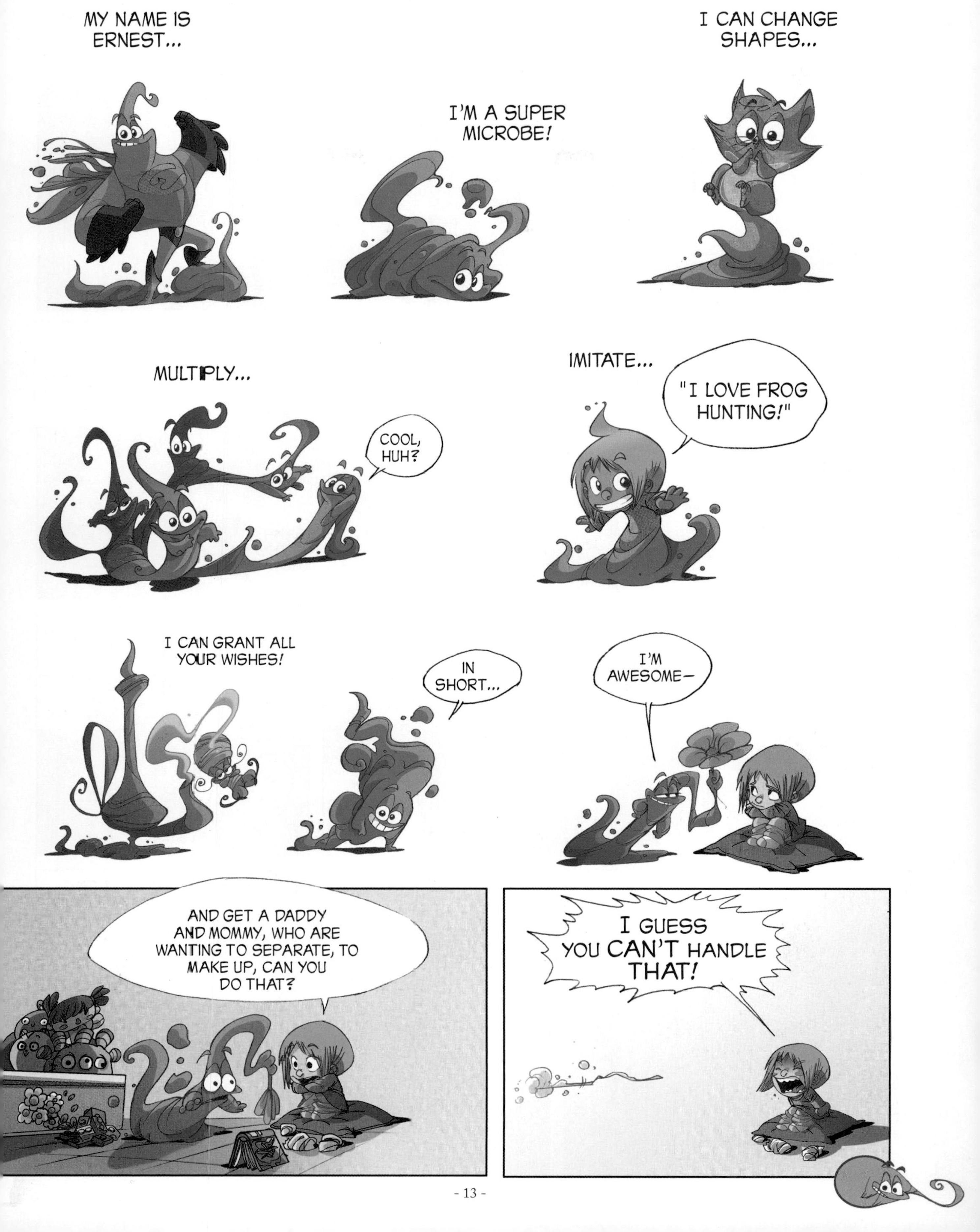

MY NAME IS ERNEST...
I'M A SUPER MICROBE!
I CAN CHANGE SHAPES...
MULTIPLY...
COOL, HUH?
IMITATE...
"I LOVE FROG HUNTING!"
I CAN GRANT ALL YOUR WISHES!
IN SHORT...
I'M AWESOME–
AND GET A DADDY AND MOMMY, WHO ARE WANTING TO SEPARATE, TO MAKE UP, CAN YOU DO THAT?
I GUESS YOU CAN'T HANDLE THAT!

UNFORTUNATELY, REBECCA THE INTREPID FROG HUNTER HAS GOTTEN LOST IN THE SEWERS...

AN ACRID, TOXIC SMELL OF SULFUR AND TRASH CRUELLY ASSAULTED HER NOSTRILS...

SHE'S STARTING TO RUN SERIOUSLY SHORT OF AIR... THE SITUATION IS CRITICAL...

BUT SUDDENLY HOPE BUBBLES TO THE SURFACE...

ERDEST!

QUICK, KSHHH... FOWWOW ME!

ERNEST, HER FAITHFUL SIDEKICK, IS DETERMINED TO GET HER OUT OF THIS DIRE FIX...

KSSHHH-- IT'S THIS WAY!

THE WAY OUT IS CLOSE...

KEEP GOING!

I CAN'T GO ON...

I'M CHOKING...

MY EYES STING...

JUST A FEW MORE YARDS... KSSH...

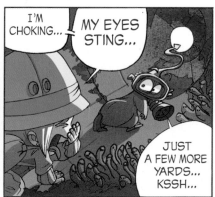

I'M GONNA THROW UP...

TAKE MY HAND! KSSHHH...

⚡COFF!⚡ ⚡COFF!⚡ THIS STUFF IS HORRIBLE! ARE YOU TRYING TO KILL ME OR WHAT?!

FINISH YOUR INHALATION TREATMENT, SWEETIE! IT'S GOOD FOR YOUR BRONCHIAL TUBES!

OOOH... WHAT A CONSIDERATE MOTHER YOU ARE!

DON'T YOU GET STARTED, OKAY!

HELLO, DR. FAKBERT! THANK YOU FOR COMING SO QUICKLY!

HOW'S OUR LITTLE PATIENT?

SHE CAUGHT A COLD, DOCTOR, I'M WORRIED...

SHE'S SO VULNERABLE... IF ONLY...

COME, COME, NO WORRYING, I'M HERE...

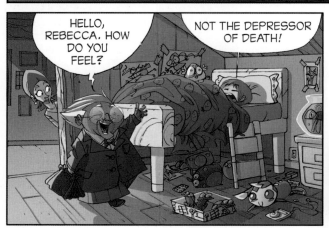

HELLO, REBECCA. HOW DO YOU FEEL?

NOT THE DEPRESSOR OF DEATH!

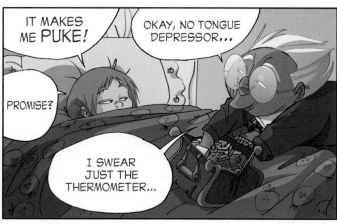

IT MAKES ME PUKE!

OKAY, NO TONGUE DEPRESSOR...

PROMISE?

I SWEAR JUST THE THERMOMETER...

I SWEAR IT ON THE HIPPOCRATIC OATH!

HIPPO WHAT?

SHHHHH... THERE... THAT'S GOOD...

99.5 DEGREES... HMM...

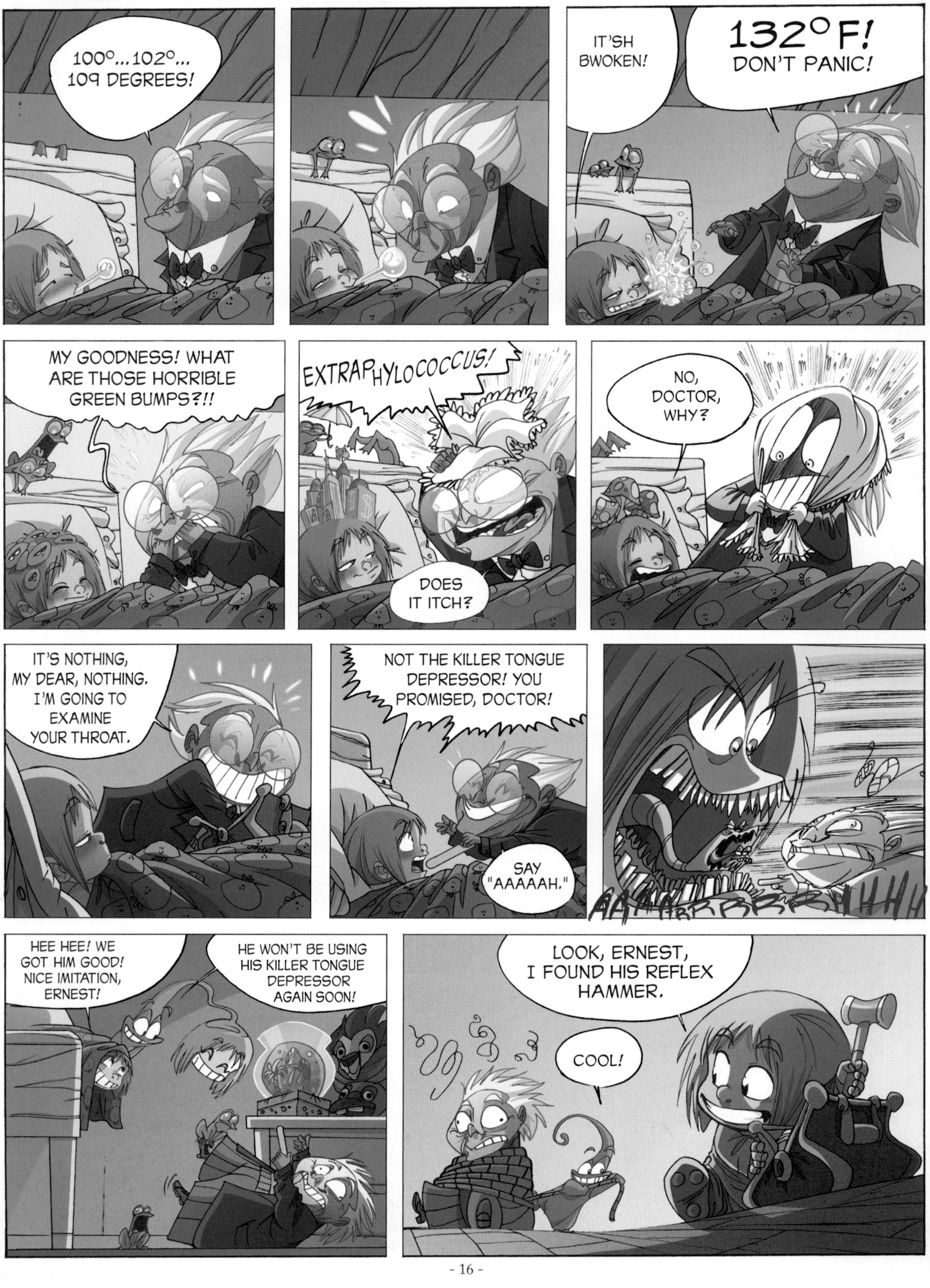
100°...102°... 109 DEGREES!
IT'SH BWOKEN!
132° F! DON'T PANIC!
MY GOODNESS! WHAT ARE THOSE HORRIBLE GREEN BUMPS?!!
EXTRAPHYLOCOCCUS!
DOES IT ITCH?
NO, DOCTOR, WHY?
IT'S NOTHING, MY DEAR, NOTHING. I'M GOING TO EXAMINE YOUR THROAT.
NOT THE KILLER TONGUE DEPRESSOR! YOU PROMISED, DOCTOR!
SAY "AAAAAH."
HEE HEE! WE GOT HIM GOOD! NICE IMITATION, ERNEST!
HE WON'T BE USING HIS KILLER TONGUE DEPRESSOR AGAIN SOON!
LOOK, ERNEST, I FOUND HIS REFLEX HAMMER.
COOL!

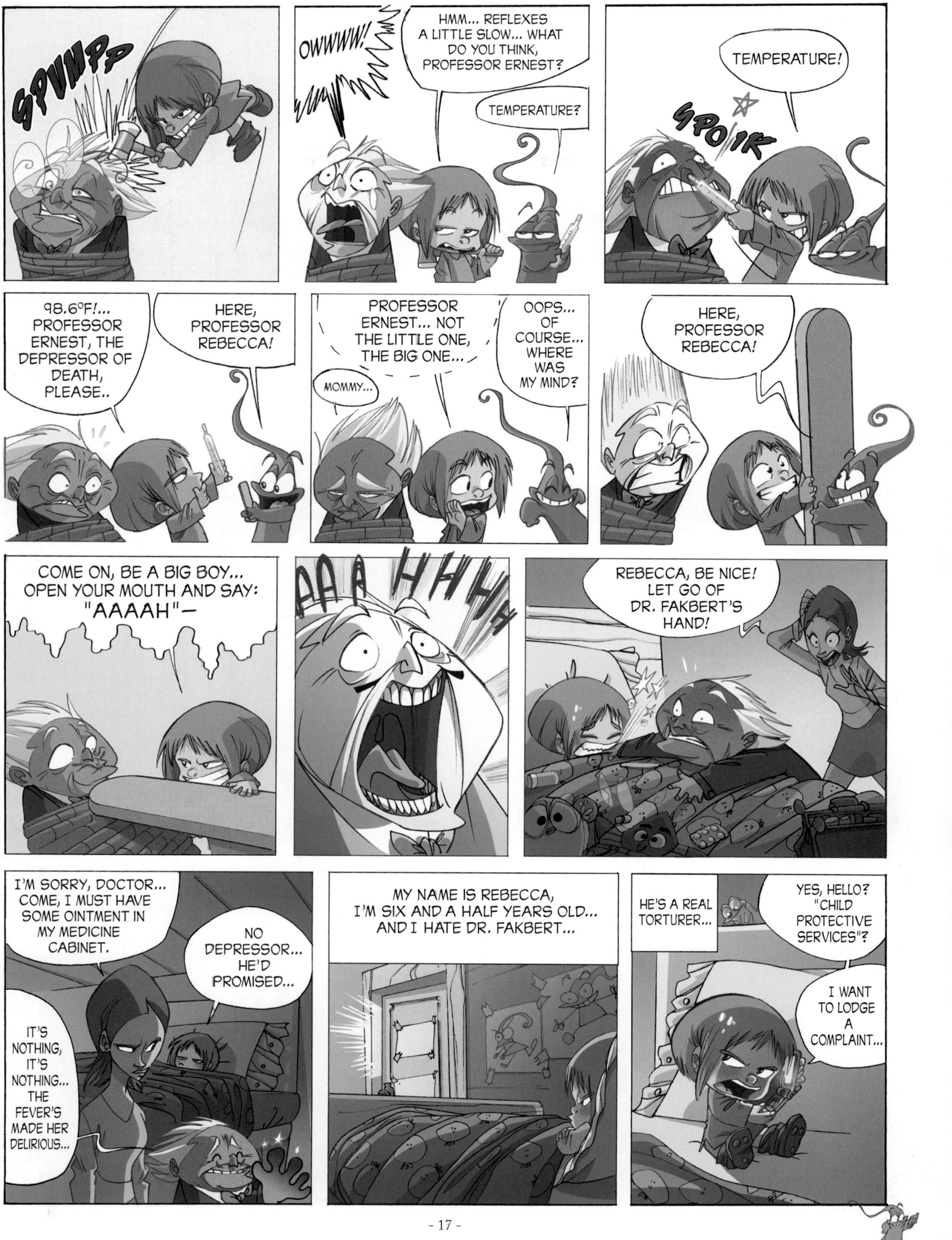
SPVMPP
OWWWW!
HMM... REFLEXES A LITTLE SLOW... WHAT DO YOU THINK, PROFESSOR ERNEST?
TEMPERATURE?
TEMPERATURE!
SPO//IK
98.6°F!... PROFESSOR ERNEST, THE DEPRESSOR OF DEATH, PLEASE..
HERE, PROFESSOR REBECCA!
PROFESSOR ERNEST... NOT THE LITTLE ONE, THE BIG ONE...
MOMMY...
OOPS... OF COURSE... WHERE WAS MY MIND?
HERE, PROFESSOR REBECCA!
COME ON, BE A BIG BOY... OPEN YOUR MOUTH AND SAY: "AAAAH"—
AAAHHHH
REBECCA, BE NICE! LET GO OF DR. FAKBERT'S HAND!
I'M SORRY, DOCTOR... COME, I MUST HAVE SOME OINTMENT IN MY MEDICINE CABINET.
NO DEPRESSOR... HE'D PROMISED...
IT'S NOTHING, IT'S NOTHING... THE FEVER'S MADE HER DELIRIOUS...
MY NAME IS REBECCA, I'M SIX AND A HALF YEARS OLD... AND I HATE DR. FAKBERT...
HE'S A REAL TORTURER...
YES, HELLO? "CHILD PROTECTIVE SERVICES"?
I WANT TO LODGE A COMPLAINT...

REBECCA, THE FAMOUS
FROG HUNTER IS
CAUGHT IN A TRAP...

SOMEONE TRIED TO
POISON HER!

A DISGUSTING,
BITTER TASTE COATS
HER MOUTH...

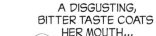

QUICK! THERE'S
ONLY ONE POSSIBLE
ANTIDOTE!

KETCHUP,
PLEEEEEASE!

TOO LATE...
HER FINAL HOUR
IS AT HAND...

PLOP!

COME ON,
MUNCHKIN...
DON'T YOU THINK
YOU'RE
EXAGGERATING
A LITTLE
BIT?

IT'S JUST
COUGH
SYRUP!

I AIN'T
NO
"MUNCHKIN"!

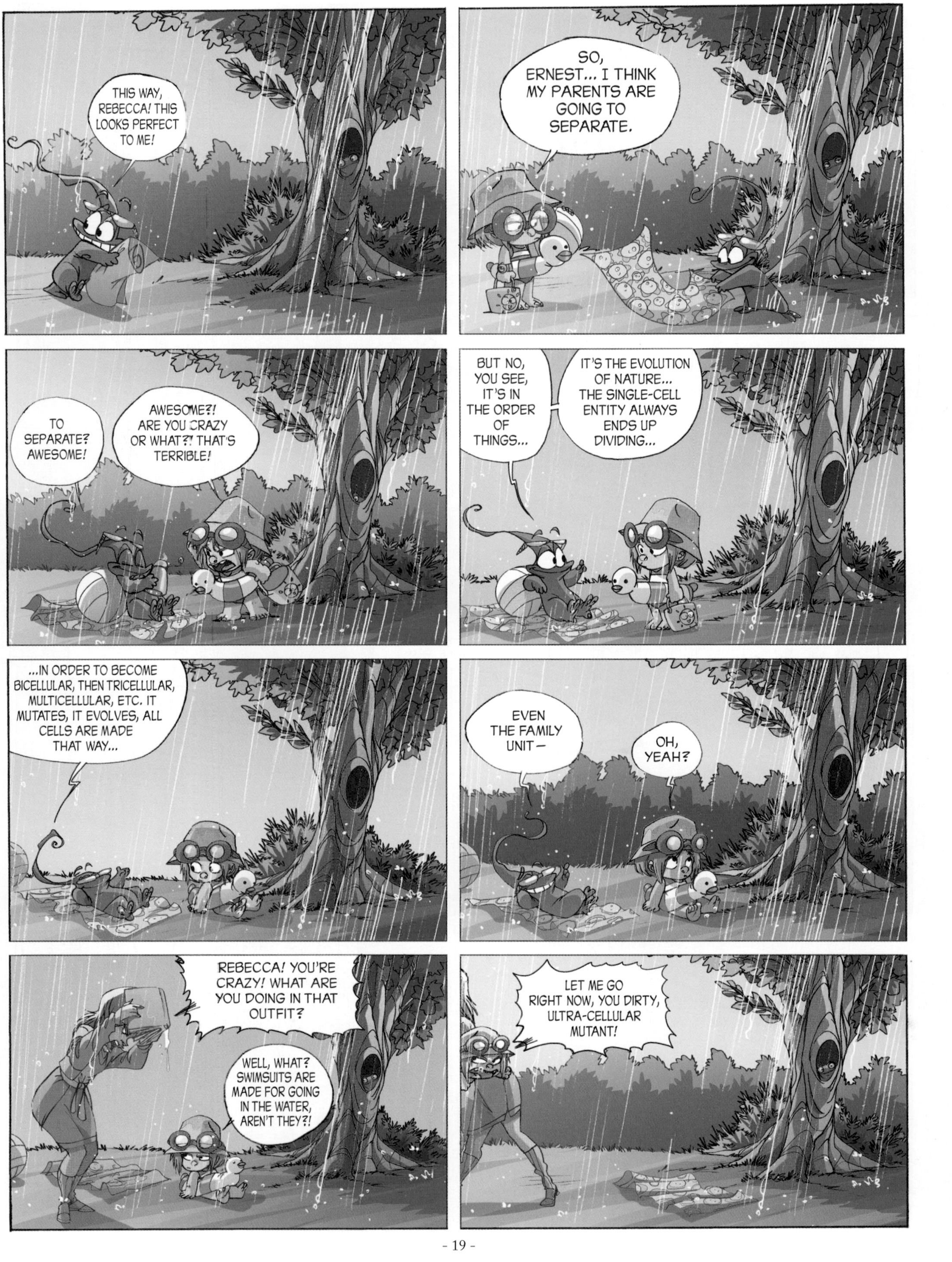
THIS WAY, REBECCA! THIS LOOKS PERFECT TO ME!
SO, ERNEST... I THINK MY PARENTS ARE GOING TO SEPARATE.
TO SEPARATE? AWESOME!
AWESOME?! ARE YOU CRAZY OR WHAT?! THAT'S TERRIBLE!
BUT NO, YOU SEE, IT'S IN THE ORDER OF THINGS...
IT'S THE EVOLUTION OF NATURE... THE SINGLE-CELL ENTITY ALWAYS ENDS UP DIVIDING...
...IN ORDER TO BECOME BICELLULAR, THEN TRICELLULAR, MULTICELLULAR, ETC. IT MUTATES, IT EVOLVES, ALL CELLS ARE MADE THAT WAY...
EVEN THE FAMILY UNIT—
OH, YEAH?
REBECCA! YOU'RE CRAZY! WHAT ARE YOU DOING IN THAT OUTFIT?
WELL, WHAT? SWIMSUITS ARE MADE FOR GOING IN THE WATER, AREN'T THEY?!
LET ME GO RIGHT NOW, YOU DIRTY, ULTRA-CELLULAR MUTANT!

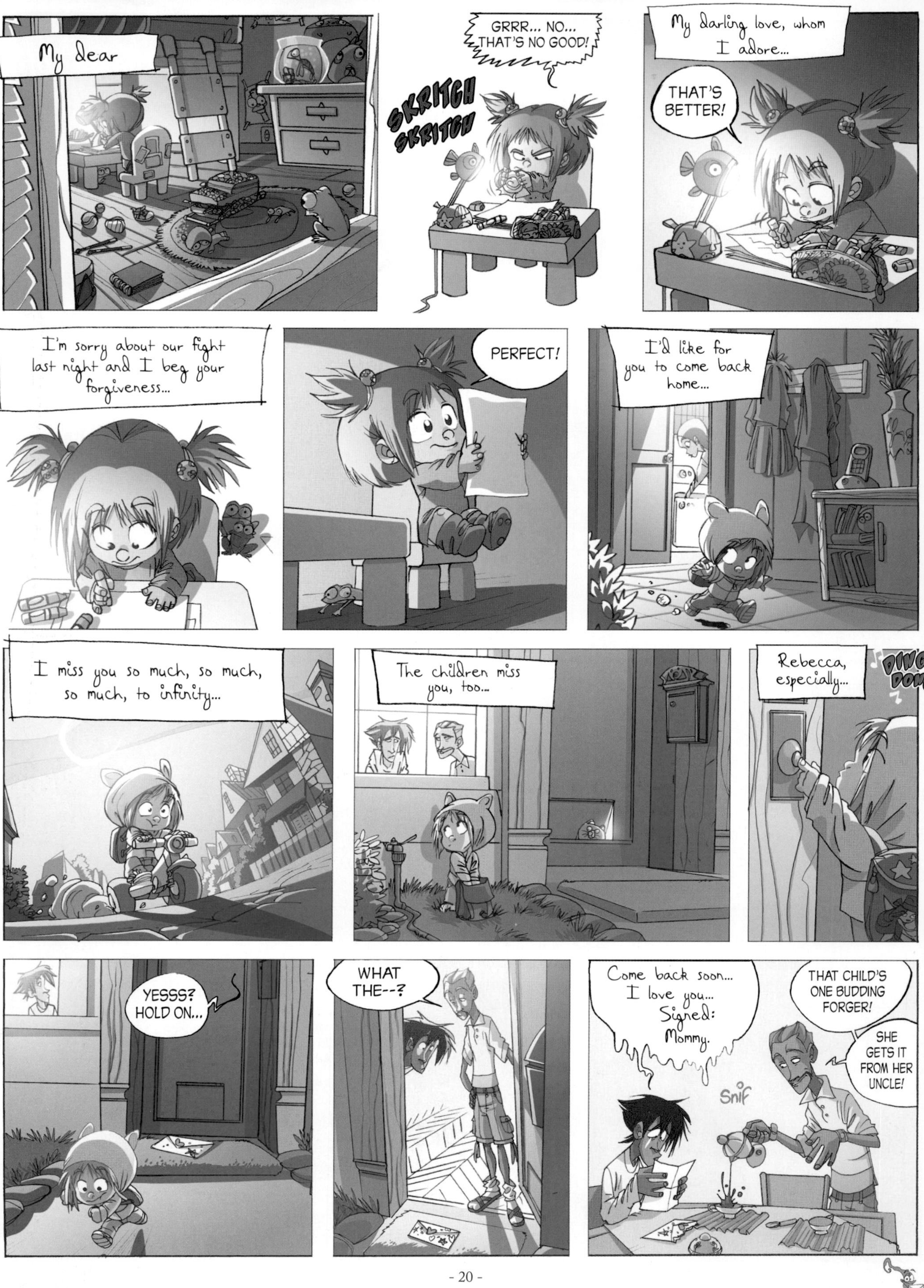
My dear
GRRR... NO... THAT'S NO GOOD!
SKRITCH SKRITCH
My darling love, whom I adore...
THAT'S BETTER!
I'm sorry about our fight last night and I beg your forgiveness...
PERFECT!
I'd like for you to come back home...
I miss you so much, so much, so much, to infinity...
The children miss you, too...
Rebecca, especially...
DING DONG
YESSS? HOLD ON...
WHAT THE--?
Come back soon... I love you... Signed: Mommy.
THAT CHILD'S ONE BUDDING FORGER!
SHE GETS IT FROM HER UNCLE!
SNIF

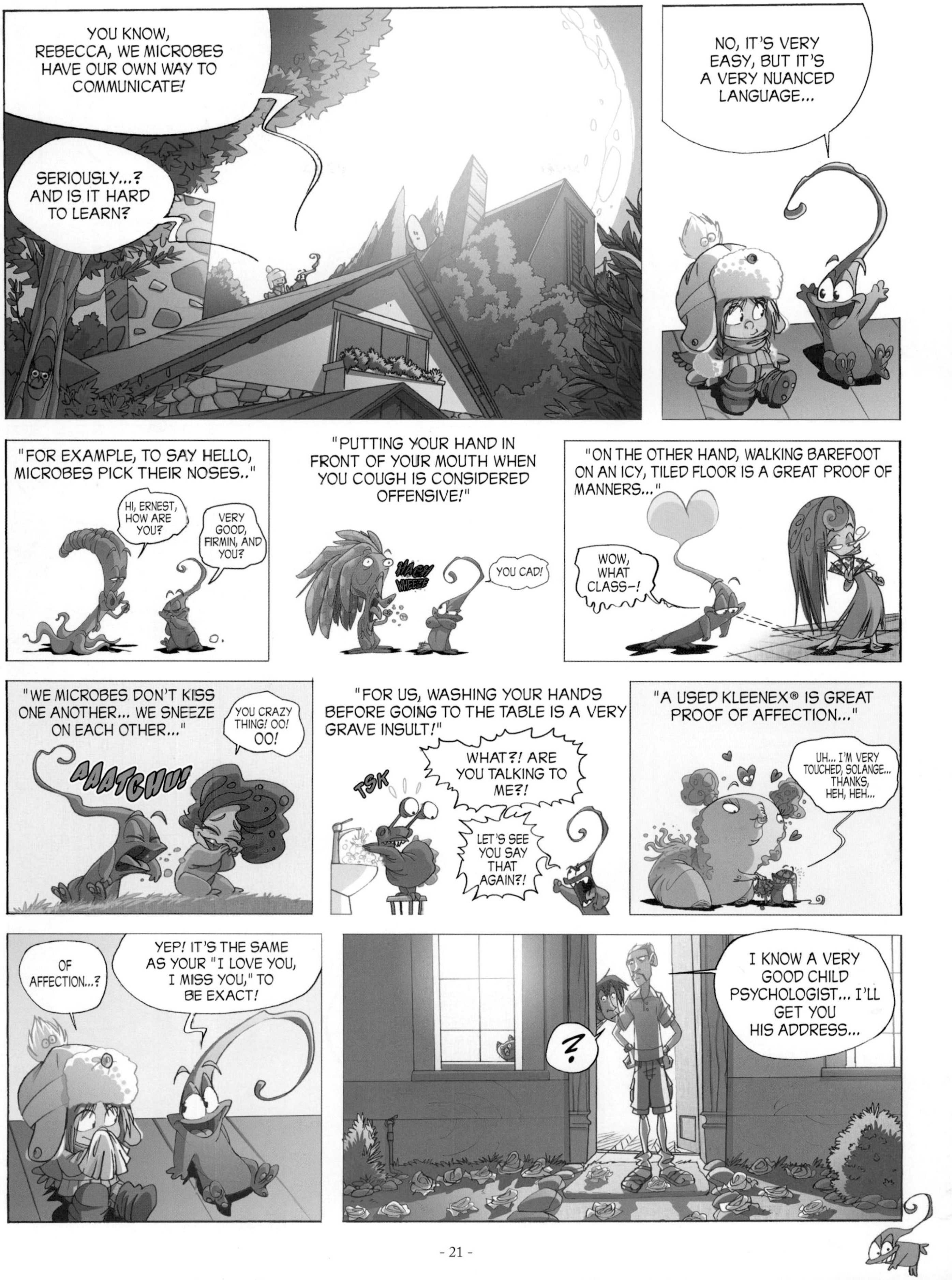
YOU KNOW, REBECCA, WE MICROBES HAVE OUR OWN WAY TO COMMUNICATE!
SERIOUSLY...? AND IS IT HARD TO LEARN?
NO, IT'S VERY EASY, BUT IT'S A VERY NUANCED LANGUAGE...
"FOR EXAMPLE, TO SAY HELLO, MICROBES PICK THEIR NOSES.."
HI, ERNEST, HOW ARE YOU?
VERY GOOD, FIRMIN, AND YOU?
"PUTTING YOUR HAND IN FRONT OF YOUR MOUTH WHEN YOU COUGH IS CONSIDERED OFFENSIVE!"
HACH
WHEEZE
YOU CAD!
"ON THE OTHER HAND, WALKING BAREFOOT ON AN ICY, TILED FLOOR IS A GREAT PROOF OF MANNERS..."
WOW, WHAT CLASS-!
"WE MICROBES DON'T KISS ONE ANOTHER... WE SNEEZE ON EACH OTHER..."
AAATCHU!
YOU CRAZY THING! OO! OO!
"FOR US, WASHING YOUR HANDS BEFORE GOING TO THE TABLE IS A VERY GRAVE INSULT!"
TSK
WHAT?! ARE YOU TALKING TO ME?!
LET'S SEE YOU SAY THAT AGAIN?!
"A USED KLEENEX® IS GREAT PROOF OF AFFECTION..."
UH... I'M VERY TOUCHED, SOLANGE... THANKS, HEH, HEH...
OF AFFECTION...?
YEP! IT'S THE SAME AS YOUR "I LOVE YOU, I MISS YOU," TO BE EXACT!
?
I KNOW A VERY GOOD CHILD PSYCHOLOGIST... I'LL GET YOU HIS ADDRESS...

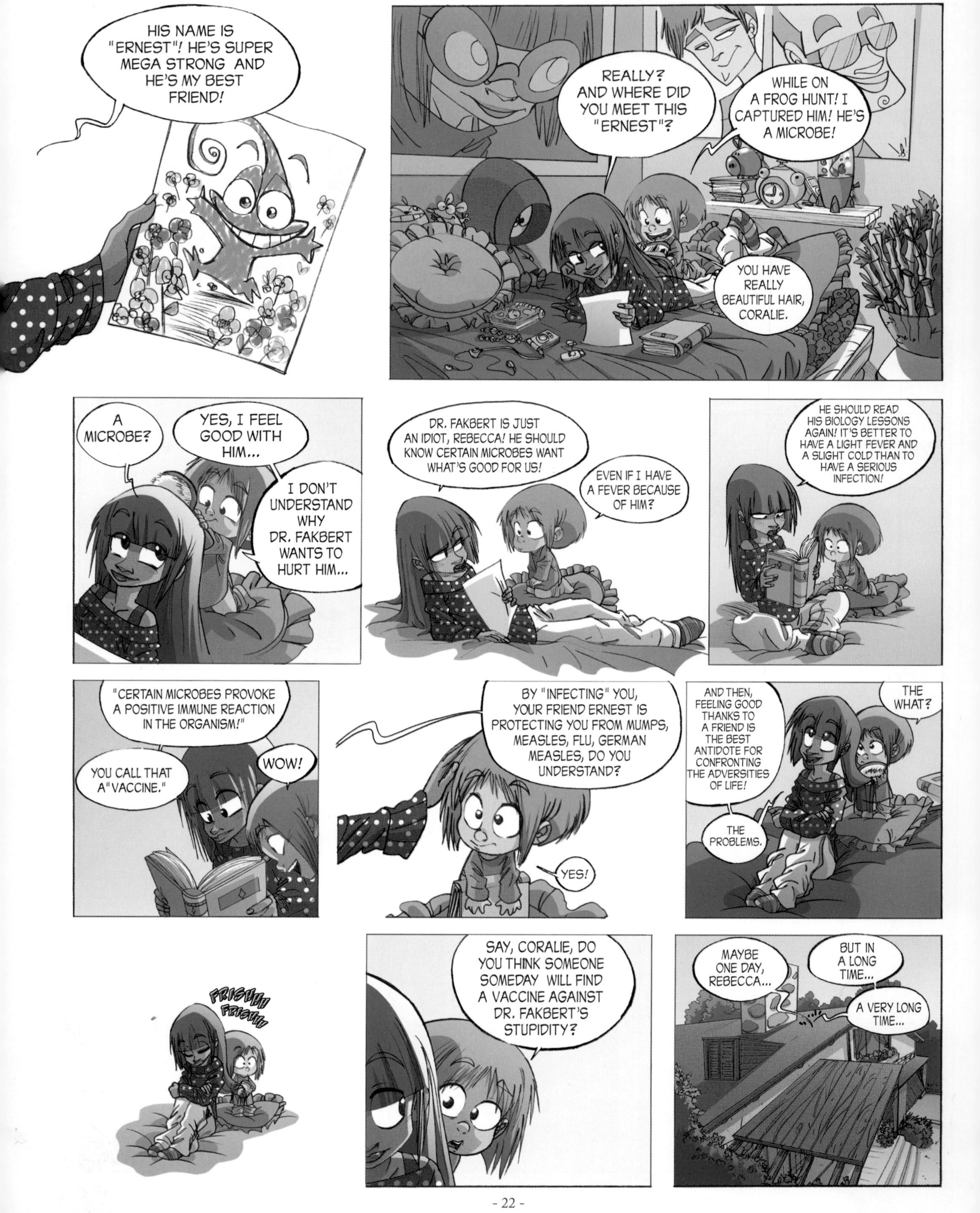
HIS NAME IS "ERNEST"! HE'S SUPER MEGA STRONG AND HE'S MY BEST FRIEND!
REALLY? AND WHERE DID YOU MEET THIS "ERNEST"?
WHILE ON A FROG HUNT! I CAPTURED HIM! HE'S A MICROBE!
YOU HAVE REALLY BEAUTIFUL HAIR, CORALIE.
A MICROBE?
YES, I FEEL GOOD WITH HIM...
I DON'T UNDERSTAND WHY DR. FAKBERT WANTS TO HURT HIM...
DR. FAKBERT IS JUST AN IDIOT, REBECCA! HE SHOULD KNOW CERTAIN MICROBES WANT WHAT'S GOOD FOR US!
EVEN IF I HAVE A FEVER BECAUSE OF HIM?
HE SHOULD READ HIS BIOLOGY LESSONS AGAIN! IT'S BETTER TO HAVE A LIGHT FEVER AND A SLIGHT COLD THAN TO HAVE A SERIOUS INFECTION!
"CERTAIN MICROBES PROVOKE A POSITIVE IMMUNE REACTION IN THE ORGANISM!"
YOU CALL THAT A "VACCINE."
WOW!
BY "INFECTING" YOU, YOUR FRIEND ERNEST IS PROTECTING YOU FROM MUMPS, MEASLES, FLU, GERMAN MEASLES, DO YOU UNDERSTAND?
YES!
AND THEN, FEELING GOOD THANKS TO A FRIEND IS THE BEST ANTIDOTE FOR CONFRONTING THE ADVERSITIES OF LIFE!
THE WHAT?
THE PROBLEMS.
SAY, CORALIE, DO YOU THINK SOMEONE SOMEDAY WILL FIND A VACCINE AGAINST DR. FAKBERT'S STUPIDITY?
MAYBE ONE DAY, REBECCA...
BUT IN A LONG TIME...
A VERY LONG TIME...

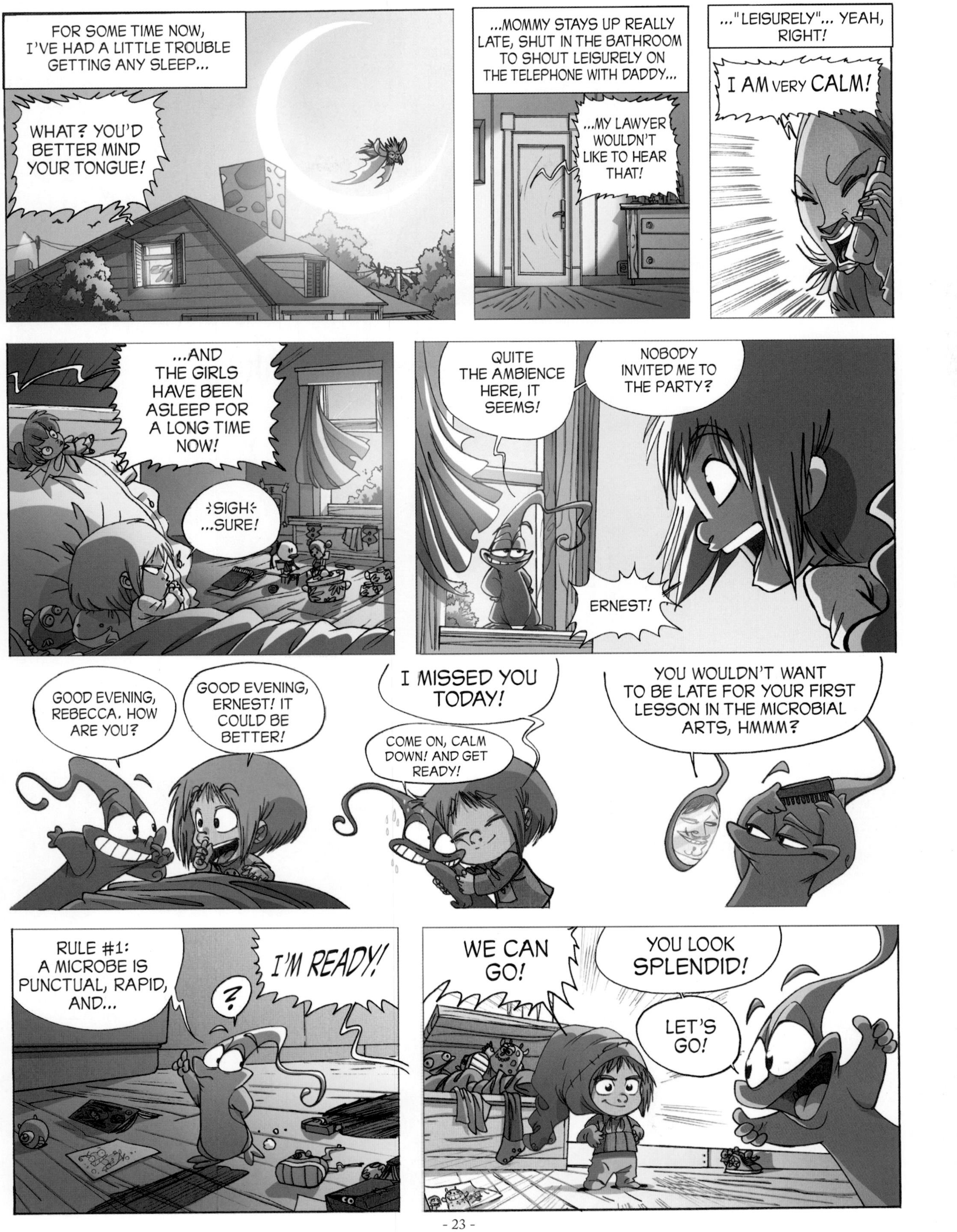
FOR SOME TIME NOW, I'VE HAD A LITTLE TROUBLE GETTING ANY SLEEP...
WHAT? YOU'D BETTER MIND YOUR TONGUE!
...MOMMY STAYS UP REALLY LATE, SHUT IN THE BATHROOM TO SHOUT LEISURELY ON THE TELEPHONE WITH DADDY...
...MY LAWYER WOULDN'T LIKE TO HEAR THAT!
..."LEISURELY"... YEAH, RIGHT!
I AM VERY CALM!
...AND THE GIRLS HAVE BEEN ASLEEP FOR A LONG TIME NOW!
SIGH ...SURE!
QUITE THE AMBIENCE HERE, IT SEEMS!
NOBODY INVITED ME TO THE PARTY?
ERNEST!
GOOD EVENING, REBECCA. HOW ARE YOU?
GOOD EVENING, ERNEST! IT COULD BE BETTER!
I MISSED YOU TODAY!
COME ON, CALM DOWN! AND GET READY!
YOU WOULDN'T WANT TO BE LATE FOR YOUR FIRST LESSON IN THE MICROBIAL ARTS, HMMM?
RULE #1: A MICROBE IS PUNCTUAL, RAPID, AND...
I'M READY!
?
WE CAN GO!
YOU LOOK SPLENDID!
LET'S GO!

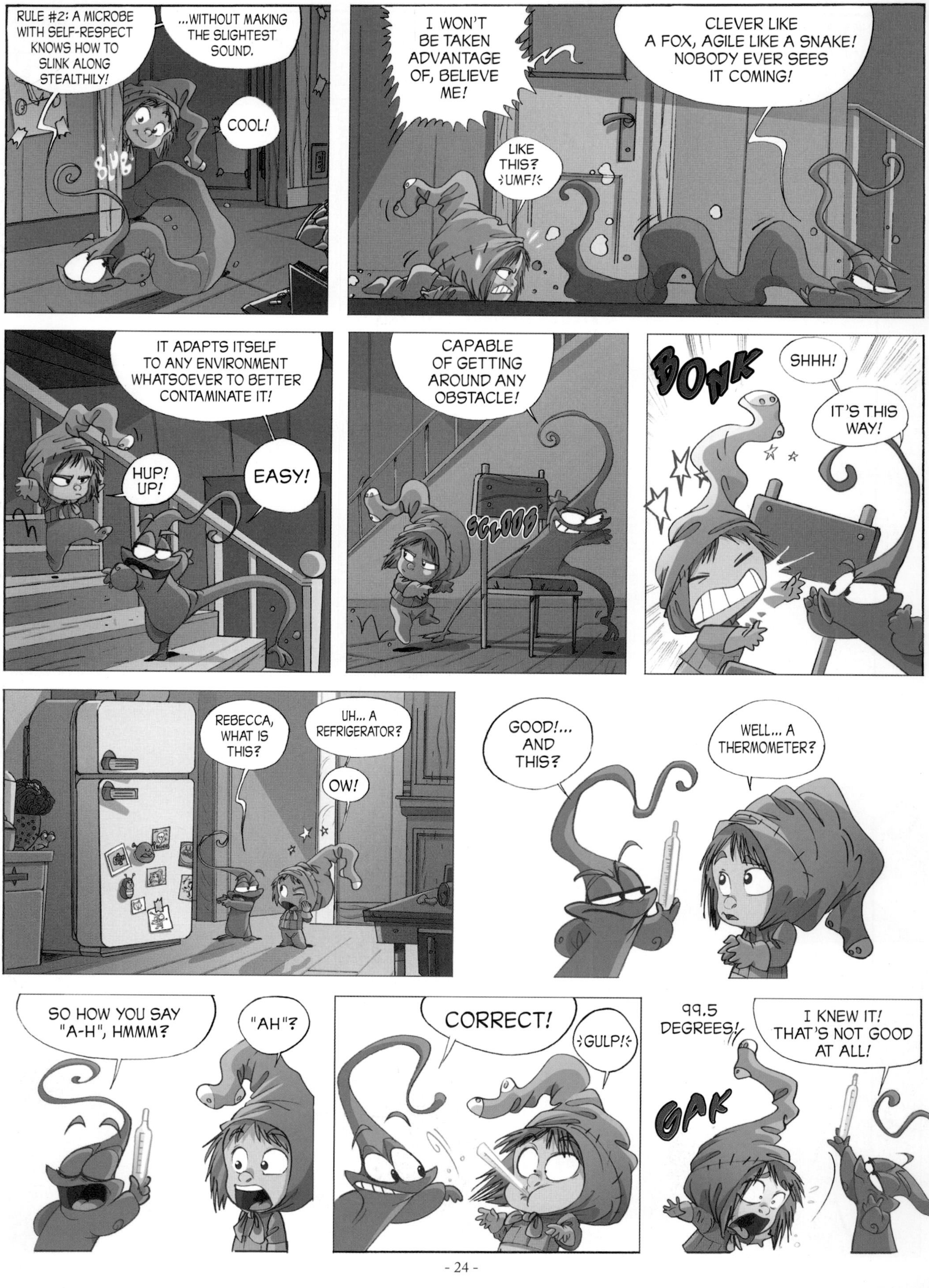
RULE #2: A MICROBE WITH SELF-RESPECT KNOWS HOW TO SLINK ALONG STEALTHILY!
...WITHOUT MAKING THE SLIGHTEST SOUND.
COOL!
I WON'T BE TAKEN ADVANTAGE OF, BELIEVE ME!
CLEVER LIKE A FOX, AGILE LIKE A SNAKE! NOBODY EVER SEES IT COMING!
LIKE THIS? UMF!
IT ADAPTS ITSELF TO ANY ENVIRONMENT WHATSOEVER TO BETTER CONTAMINATE IT!
HUP! UP!
EASY!
CAPABLE OF GETTING AROUND ANY OBSTACLE!
BONK
SHHH!
IT'S THIS WAY!
REBECCA, WHAT IS THIS?
UH... A REFRIGERATOR?
OW!
GOOD!... AND THIS?
WELL... A THERMOMETER?
SO HOW YOU SAY "A-H", HMMM?
"AH"?
CORRECT!
GULP!
99.5 DEGREES!
I KNEW IT! THAT'S NOT GOOD AT ALL!
GAK

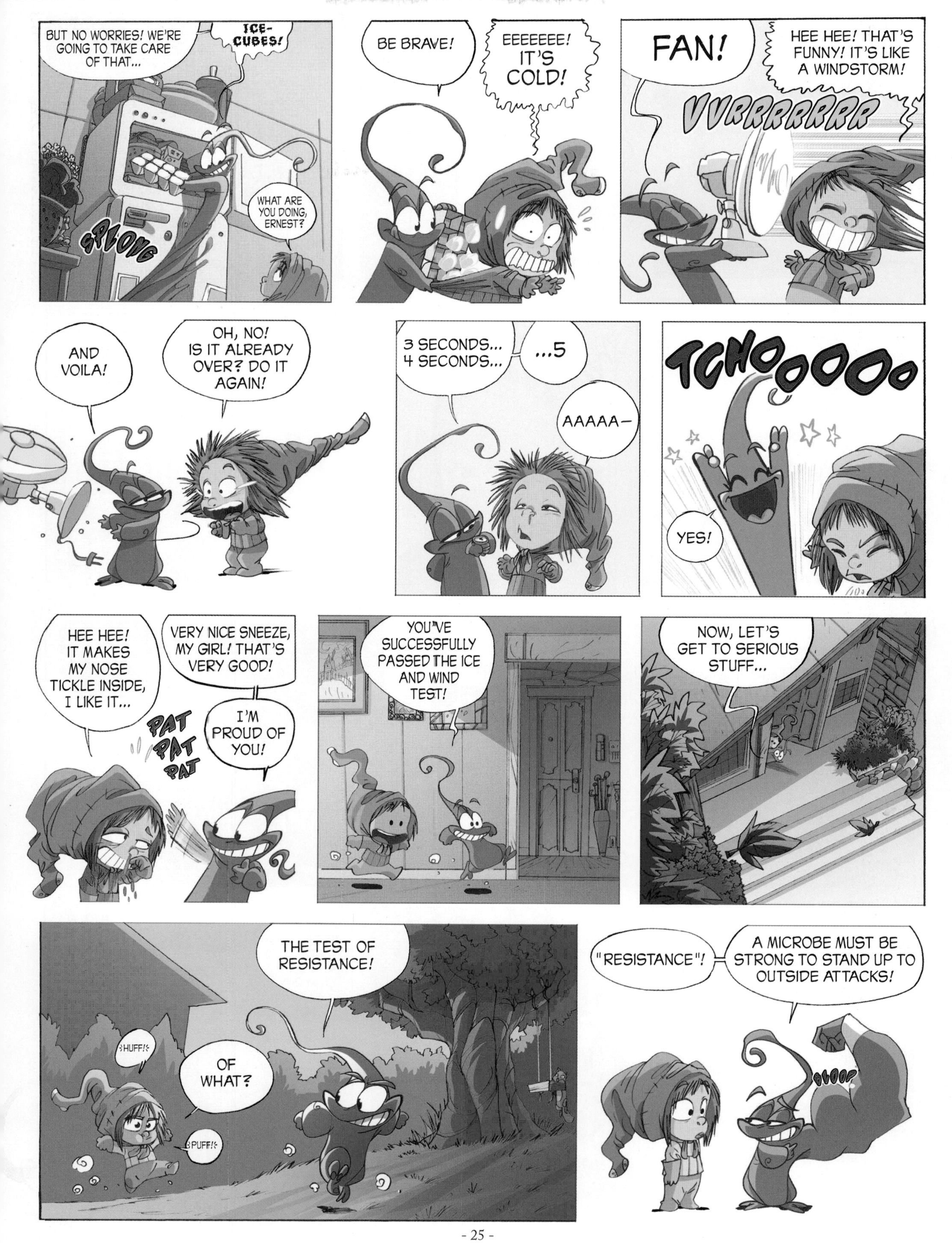
BUT NO WORRIES! WE'RE GOING TO TAKE CARE OF THAT...
ICE-CUBES!
SPLONG
WHAT ARE YOU DOING, ERNEST?
BE BRAVE!
EEEEEEE! IT'S COLD!
FAN!
HEE HEE! THAT'S FUNNY! IT'S LIKE A WINDSTORM!
VVRRRRRRR
AND VOILA!
OH, NO! IS IT ALREADY OVER? DO IT AGAIN!
3 SECONDS... 4 SECONDS...
...5
AAAAA–
TCHOOOOOO
YES!
HEE HEE! IT MAKES MY NOSE TICKLE INSIDE, I LIKE IT...
VERY NICE SNEEZE, MY GIRL! THAT'S VERY GOOD!
PAT PAT PAT
I'M PROUD OF YOU!
YOU'VE SUCCESSFULLY PASSED THE ICE AND WIND TEST!
NOW, LET'S GET TO SERIOUS STUFF...
THE TEST OF RESISTANCE!
HUFF!
OF WHAT?
PUFF!
"RESISTANCE"!
A MICROBE MUST BE STRONG TO STAND UP TO OUTSIDE ATTACKS!
BLOOP

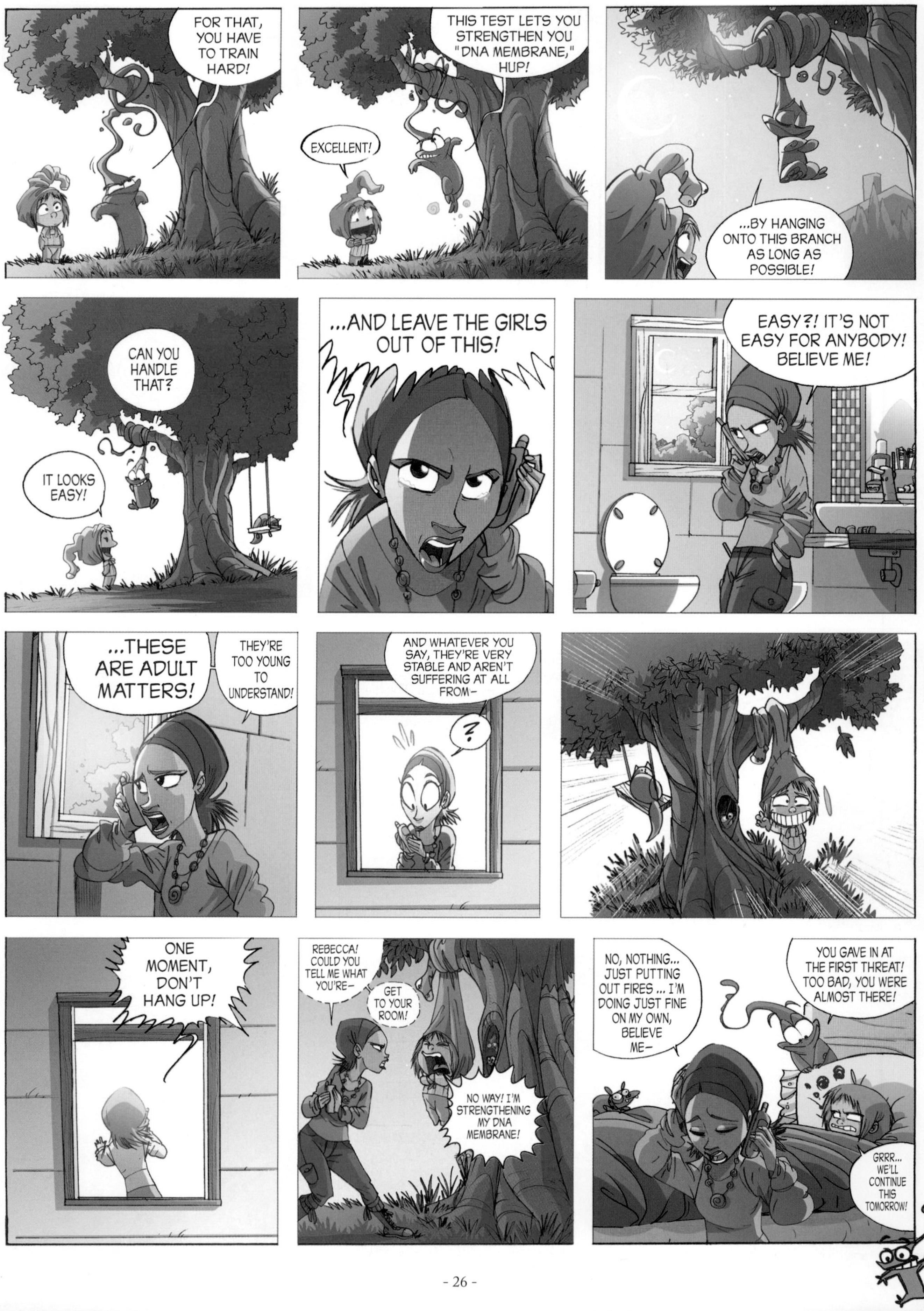
FOR THAT, YOU HAVE TO TRAIN HARD!
THIS TEST LETS YOU STRENGTHEN YOU "DNA MEMBRANE," HUP!
EXCELLENT!
...BY HANGING ONTO THIS BRANCH AS LONG AS POSSIBLE!
CAN YOU HANDLE THAT?
IT LOOKS EASY!
...AND LEAVE THE GIRLS OUT OF THIS!
EASY?! IT'S NOT EASY FOR ANYBODY! BELIEVE ME!
...THESE ARE ADULT MATTERS!
THEY'RE TOO YOUNG TO UNDERSTAND!
AND WHATEVER YOU SAY, THEY'RE VERY STABLE AND AREN'T SUFFERING AT ALL FROM–
?
ONE MOMENT, DON'T HANG UP!
REBECCA! COULD YOU TELL ME WHAT YOU'RE–
GET TO YOUR ROOM!
NO WAY! I'M STRENGTHENING MY DNA MEMBRANE!
NO, NOTHING... JUST PUTTING OUT FIRES ... I'M DOING JUST FINE ON MY OWN, BELIEVE ME–
YOU GAVE IN AT THE FIRST THREAT! TOO BAD, YOU WERE ALMOST THERE!
GRRR... WE'LL CONTINUE THIS TOMORROW!

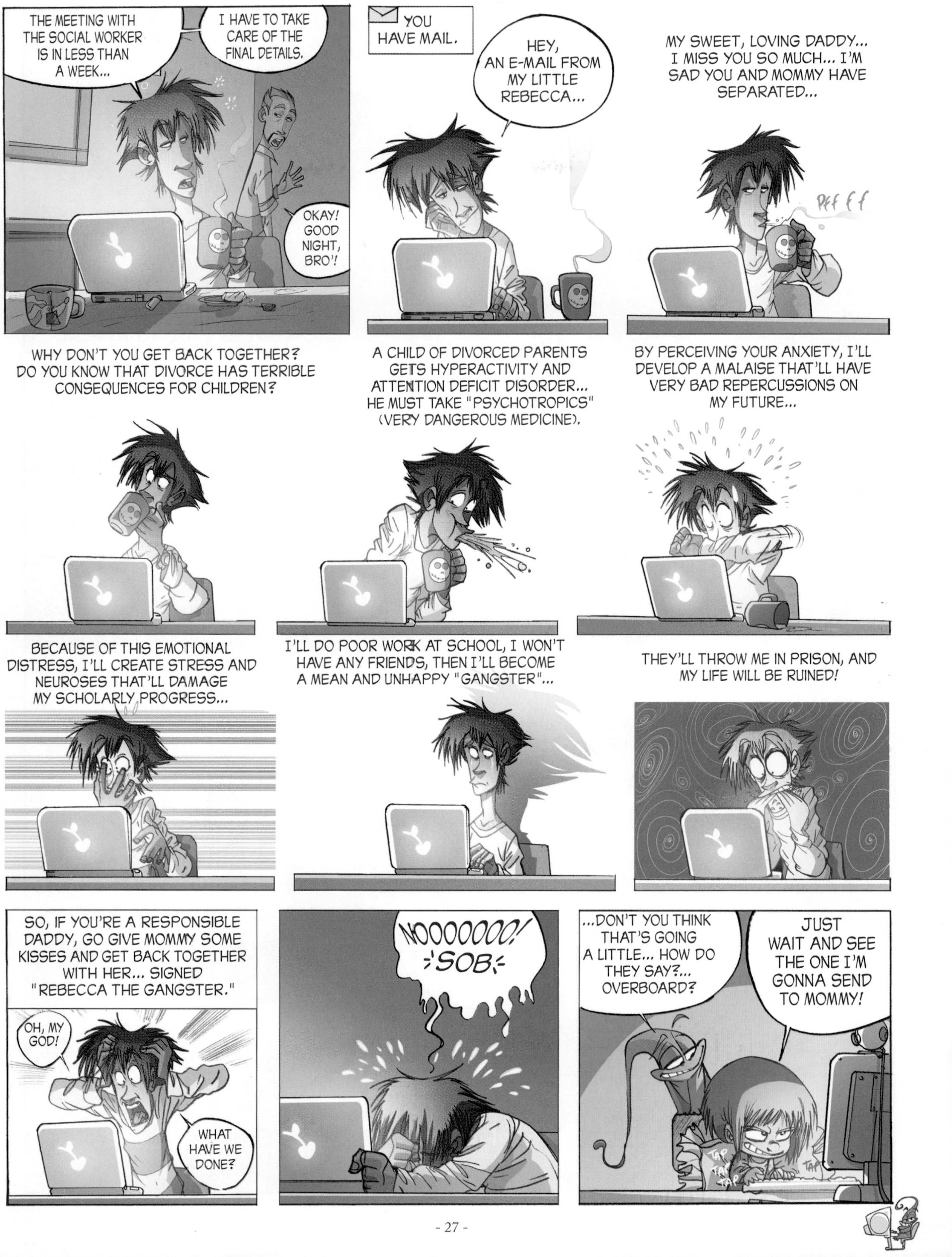

THE MEETING WITH THE SOCIAL WORKER IS IN LESS THAN A WEEK...
I HAVE TO TAKE CARE OF THE FINAL DETAILS.
OKAY! GOOD NIGHT, BRO'!
YOU HAVE MAIL.
HEY, AN E-MAIL FROM MY LITTLE REBECCA...
MY SWEET, LOVING DADDY... I MISS YOU SO MUCH... I'M SAD YOU AND MOMMY HAVE SEPARATED...
PFF F F
WHY DON'T YOU GET BACK TOGETHER? DO YOU KNOW THAT DIVORCE HAS TERRIBLE CONSEQUENCES FOR CHILDREN?
A CHILD OF DIVORCED PARENTS GETS HYPERACTIVITY AND ATTENTION DEFICIT DISORDER... HE MUST TAKE "PSYCHOTROPICS" (VERY DANGEROUS MEDICINE).
BY PERCEIVING YOUR ANXIETY, I'LL DEVELOP A MALAISE THAT'LL HAVE VERY BAD REPERCUSSIONS ON MY FUTURE...
BECAUSE OF THIS EMOTIONAL DISTRESS, I'LL CREATE STRESS AND NEUROSES THAT'LL DAMAGE MY SCHOLARLY PROGRESS...
I'LL DO POOR WORK AT SCHOOL, I WON'T HAVE ANY FRIENDS, THEN I'LL BECOME A MEAN AND UNHAPPY "GANGSTER"...
THEY'LL THROW ME IN PRISON, AND MY LIFE WILL BE RUINED!
SO, IF YOU'RE A RESPONSIBLE DADDY, GO GIVE MOMMY SOME KISSES AND GET BACK TOGETHER WITH HER... SIGNED "REBECCA THE GANGSTER."
OH, MY GOD!
WHAT HAVE WE DONE?
NOOOOOOO!
SOB
...DON'T YOU THINK THAT'S GOING A LITTLE... HOW DO THEY SAY?... OVERBOARD?
JUST WAIT AND SEE THE ONE I'M GONNA SEND TO MOMMY!
TAP TAP TAP
TAP

SCRAM, MORON! LEAVE HER ALONE OR YOU'LL HAVE TO DEAL WITH ME!

DON'T POKE YOUR NOSE INTO THIS, ERNEST, OR I'LL MAKE MINCEMEAT OUT OF YOU!

REALLY?! I'D LIKE TO SEE THAT!

GROOMF!

MISSED! HEE, HEE!

DWIPP

MISSED AGAIN! TRY HARDER, FOR GOODNESS' SAKE!

BLBLBLLL!

SSHPLAT!

ERNEST!

IS THAT ALL?! I'M CERTAIN YOU CAN DO BETTER...

BAD! BAD! BAD...

MORON!

BLOB BLOB

DEMONSTRATION—

POW

AAAAAA

PROJECTION!

WELL DONE!

ALL THAT BECAUSE OF A TINY PRICK FROM A NOTHING ROSE THORN...

THE TETANUS VIRUS IS VERY DANGEROUS, REBECCA.

IF YOU'RE NOT VACCINATED, DON'T TOUCH THORNS OR RUSTY METAL!

HERE, THE ROSE WAS FOR DADDY, BUT YOU REALLY DESERVE IT!

YOU'RE TOTALLY AWESOME!

"TOTALLY AWESOME"?! THAT SUPERLATIVE FITS ME RATHER WELL...

OKAY, SO ARE WE GOING ON A FROG HUNT?

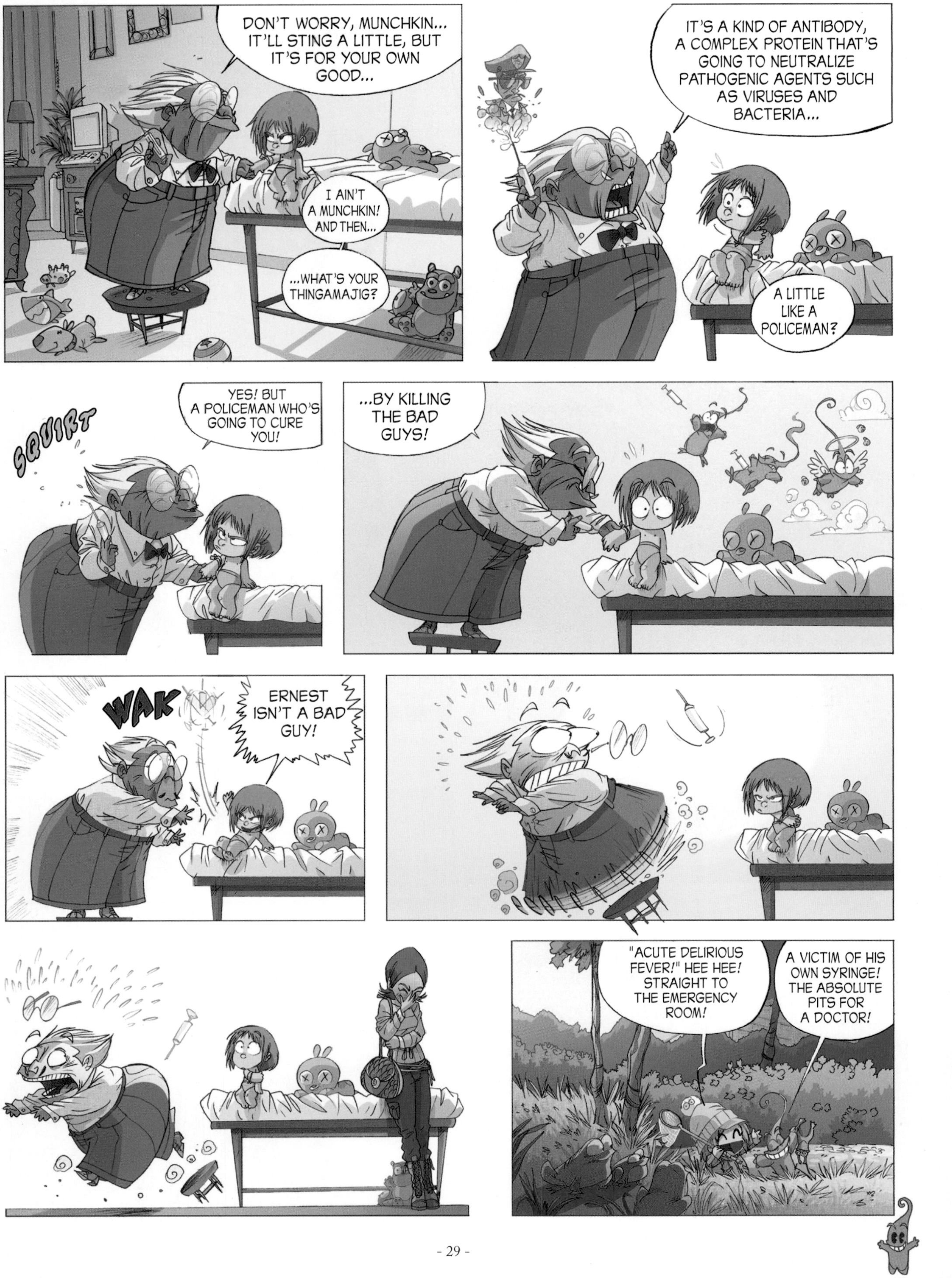
DON'T WORRY, MUNCHKIN... IT'LL STING A LITTLE, BUT IT'S FOR YOUR OWN GOOD...
I AIN'T A MUNCHKIN! AND THEN...
...WHAT'S YOUR THINGAMAJIG?
IT'S A KIND OF ANTIBODY, A COMPLEX PROTEIN THAT'S GOING TO NEUTRALIZE PATHOGENIC AGENTS SUCH AS VIRUSES AND BACTERIA...
A LITTLE LIKE A POLICEMAN?
SQUIRT
YES! BUT A POLICEMAN WHO'S GOING TO CURE YOU!
...BY KILLING THE BAD GUYS!
WAK
ERNEST ISN'T A BAD GUY!
"ACUTE DELIRIOUS FEVER!" HEE HEE! STRAIGHT TO THE EMERGENCY ROOM!
A VICTIM OF HIS OWN SYRINGE! THE ABSOLUTE PITS FOR A DOCTOR!

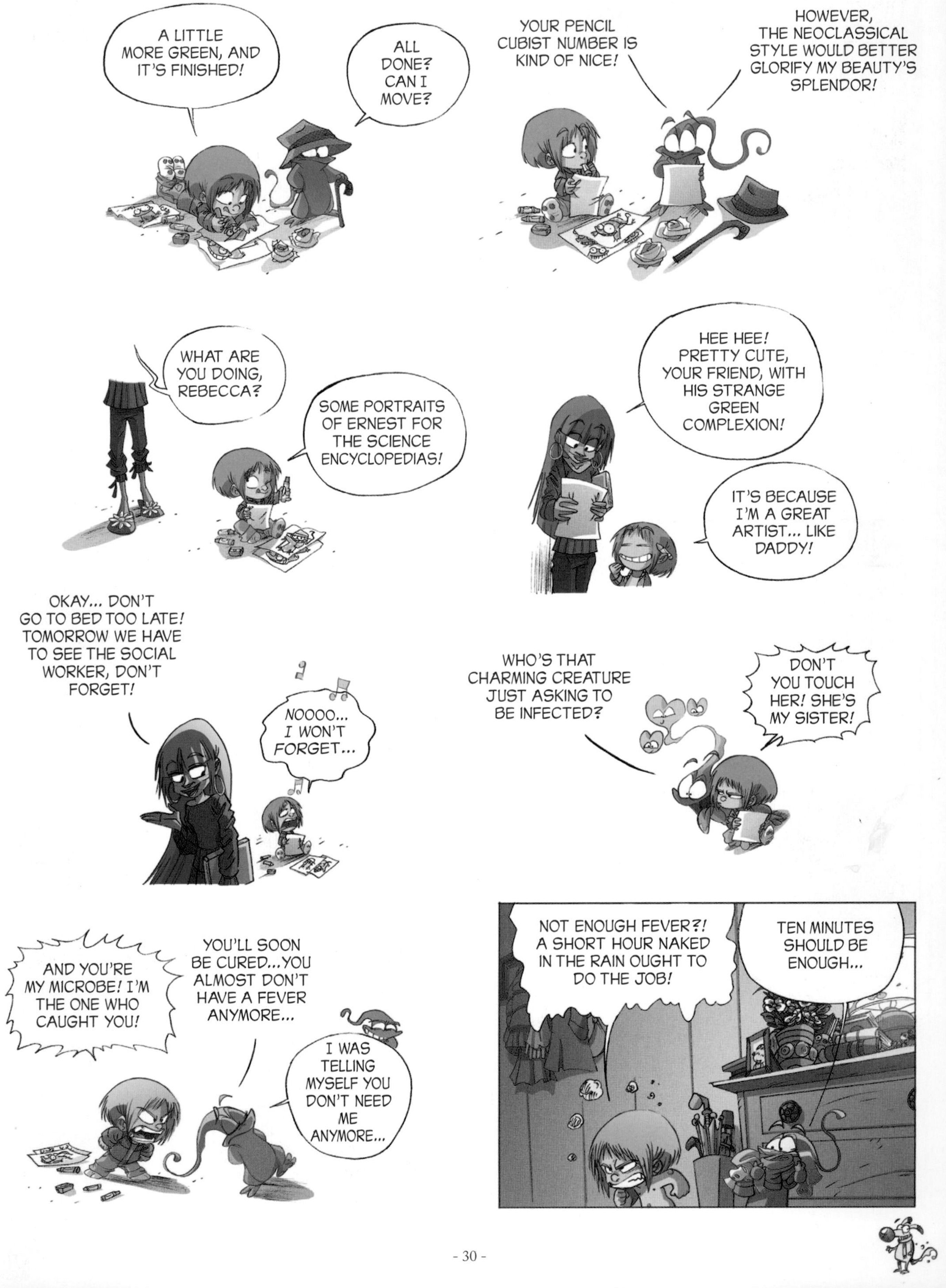
A LITTLE MORE GREEN, AND IT'S FINISHED!
ALL DONE? CAN I MOVE?
YOUR PENCIL CUBIST NUMBER IS KIND OF NICE!
HOWEVER, THE NEOCLASSICAL STYLE WOULD BETTER GLORIFY MY BEAUTY'S SPLENDOR!
WHAT ARE YOU DOING, REBECCA?
SOME PORTRAITS OF ERNEST FOR THE SCIENCE ENCYCLOPEDIAS!
HEE HEE! PRETTY CUTE, YOUR FRIEND, WITH HIS STRANGE GREEN COMPLEXION!
IT'S BECAUSE I'M A GREAT ARTIST... LIKE DADDY!
OKAY... DON'T GO TO BED TOO LATE! TOMORROW WE HAVE TO SEE THE SOCIAL WORKER, DON'T FORGET!
NOOOO... I WON'T FORGET...
WHO'S THAT CHARMING CREATURE JUST ASKING TO BE INFECTED?
DON'T YOU TOUCH HER! SHE'S MY SISTER!
YOU'LL SOON BE CURED...YOU ALMOST DON'T HAVE A FEVER ANYMORE...
AND YOU'RE MY MICROBE! I'M THE ONE WHO CAUGHT YOU!
I WAS TELLING MYSELF YOU DON'T NEED ME ANYMORE...
NOT ENOUGH FEVER?! A SHORT HOUR NAKED IN THE RAIN OUGHT TO DO THE JOB!
TEN MINUTES SHOULD BE ENOUGH...

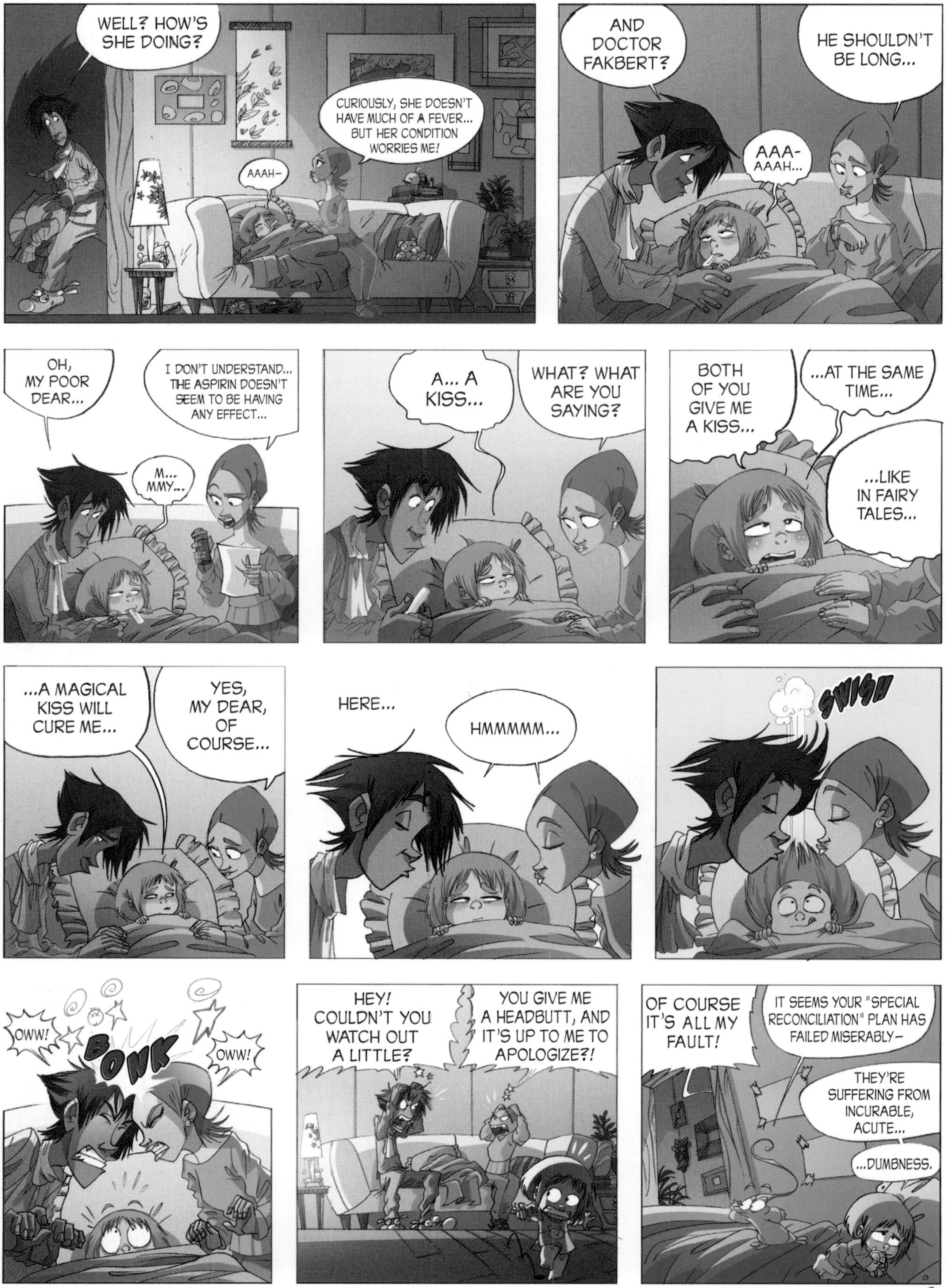
WELL? HOW'S SHE DOING?
CURIOUSLY, SHE DOESN'T HAVE MUCH OF A FEVER... BUT HER CONDITION WORRIES ME!
AAAH–
AND DOCTOR FAKBERT?
HE SHOULDN'T BE LONG...
AAA-AAAH...
OH, MY POOR DEAR...
I DON'T UNDERSTAND... THE ASPIRIN DOESN'T SEEM TO BE HAVING ANY EFFECT...
M... MMY...
A... A KISS...
WHAT? WHAT ARE YOU SAYING?
BOTH OF YOU GIVE ME A KISS...
...AT THE SAME TIME...
...LIKE IN FAIRY TALES...
...A MAGICAL KISS WILL CURE ME...
YES, MY DEAR, OF COURSE...
HERE...
HMMMMM...
SWISH
OWW!
BONK
OWW!
HEY! COULDN'T YOU WATCH OUT A LITTLE?
YOU GIVE ME A HEADBUTT, AND IT'S UP TO ME TO APOLOGIZE?!
OF COURSE IT'S ALL MY FAULT!
IT SEEMS YOUR "SPECIAL RECONCILIATION" PLAN HAS FAILED MISERABLY–
THEY'RE SUFFERING FROM INCURABLE, ACUTE...
...DUMBNESS.

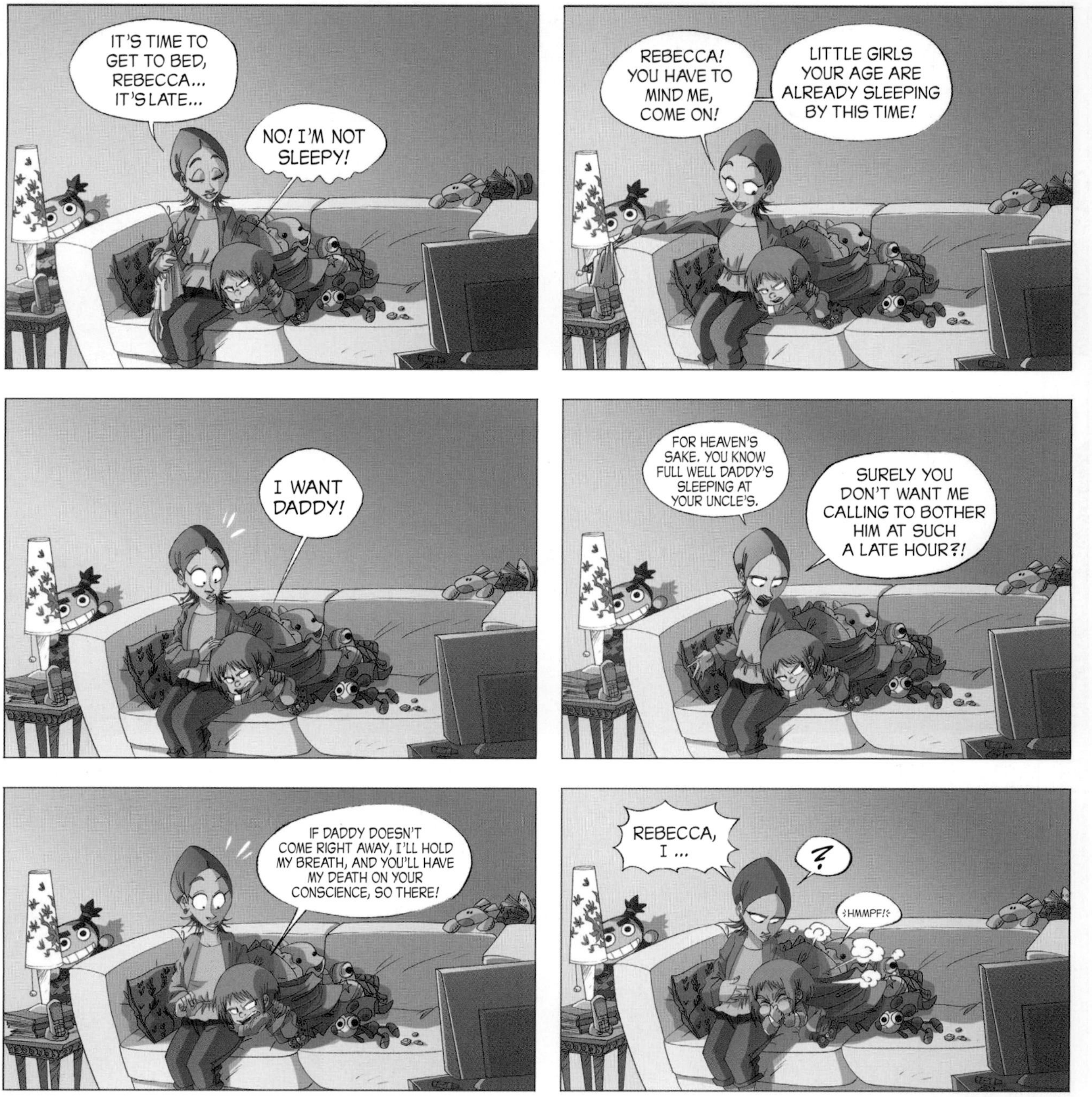
IT'S TIME TO GET TO BED, REBECCA... IT'S LATE...
NO! I'M NOT SLEEPY!
REBECCA! YOU HAVE TO MIND ME, COME ON!
LITTLE GIRLS YOUR AGE ARE ALREADY SLEEPING BY THIS TIME!
I WANT DADDY!
FOR HEAVEN'S SAKE. YOU KNOW FULL WELL DADDY'S SLEEPING AT YOUR UNCLE'S.
SURELY YOU DON'T WANT ME CALLING TO BOTHER HIM AT SUCH A LATE HOUR?!
IF DADDY DOESN'T COME RIGHT AWAY, I'LL HOLD MY BREATH, AND YOU'LL HAVE MY DEATH ON YOUR CONSCIENCE, SO THERE!
REBECCA, I ...
?
HMMPF!
WHEW! LOOKS LIKE SHE'S FINALLY FALLEN ASLEEP!
QUITE THE TEMPERAMENT, EH?
SHE GETS IT HONEST...

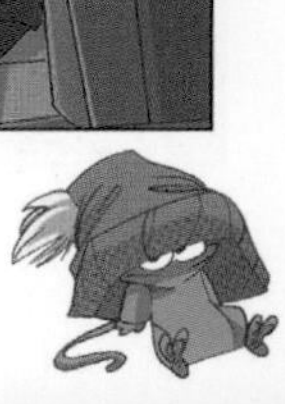

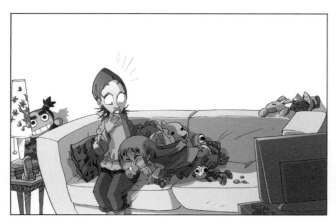

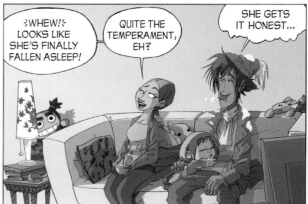

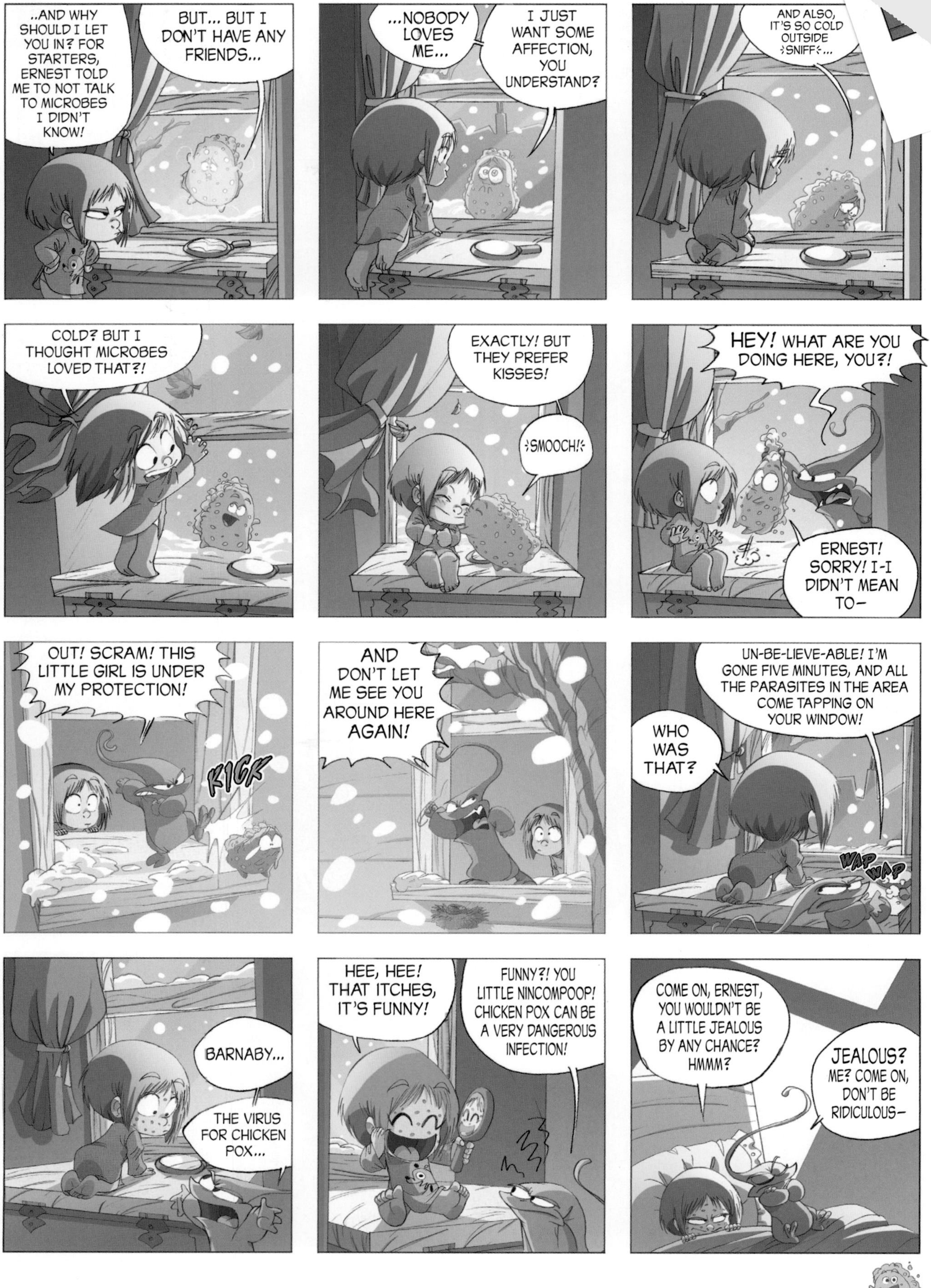
..AND WHY SHOULD I LET YOU IN? FOR STARTERS, ERNEST TOLD ME TO NOT TALK TO MICROBES I DIDN'T KNOW!
BUT... BUT I DON'T HAVE ANY FRIENDS...
...NOBODY LOVES ME...
I JUST WANT SOME AFFECTION, YOU UNDERSTAND?
AND ALSO, IT'S SO COLD OUTSIDE ⸗SNIFF⸗...
COLD? BUT I THOUGHT MICROBES LOVED THAT?!
EXACTLY! BUT THEY PREFER KISSES!
⸗SMOOCH!⸗
HEY! WHAT ARE YOU DOING HERE, YOU?!
ERNEST! SORRY! I-I DIDN'T MEAN TO—
OUT! SCRAM! THIS LITTLE GIRL IS UNDER MY PROTECTION!
KICK
AND DON'T LET ME SEE YOU AROUND HERE AGAIN!
WHO WAS THAT?
UN-BE-LIEVE-ABLE! I'M GONE FIVE MINUTES, AND ALL THE PARASITES IN THE AREA COME TAPPING ON YOUR WINDOW!
WAP WAP
BARNABY...
THE VIRUS FOR CHICKEN POX...
HEE, HEE! THAT ITCHES, IT'S FUNNY!
FUNNY?! YOU LITTLE NINCOMPOOP! CHICKEN POX CAN BE A VERY DANGEROUS INFECTION!
COME ON, ERNEST, YOU WOULDN'T BE A LITTLE JEALOUS BY ANY CHANCE? HMMM?
JEALOUS? ME? COME ON, DON'T BE RIDICULOUS—

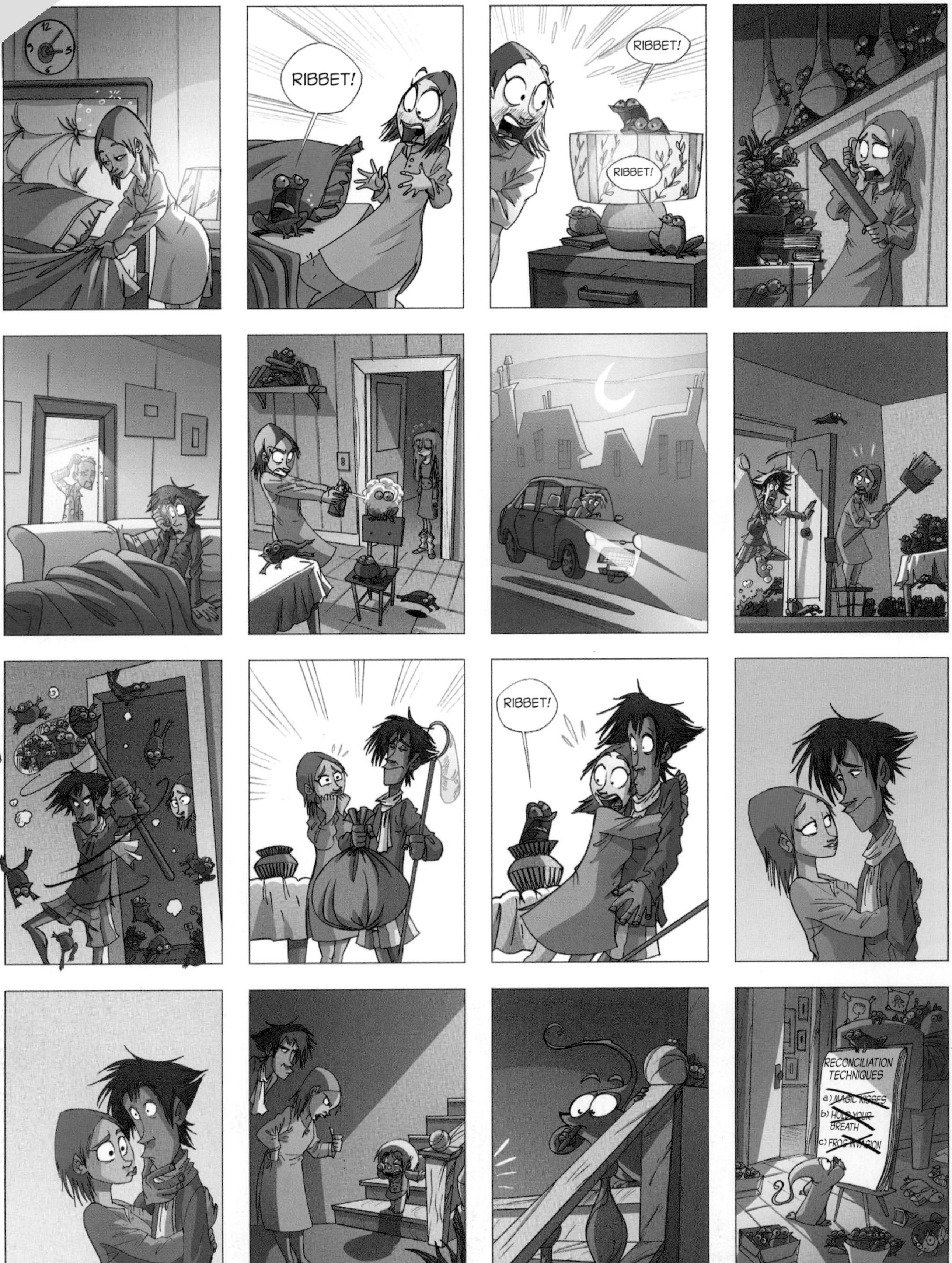
RIBBET!
RIBBET!
RIBBET!
RIBBET!
RECONCILIATION TECHNIQUES
a) MAGIC KISSES
b) HOLD YOUR BREATH
c) FROG INVASION

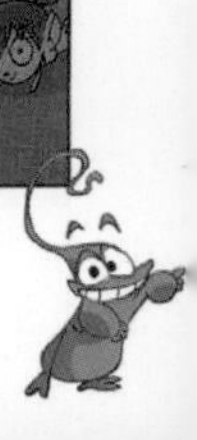

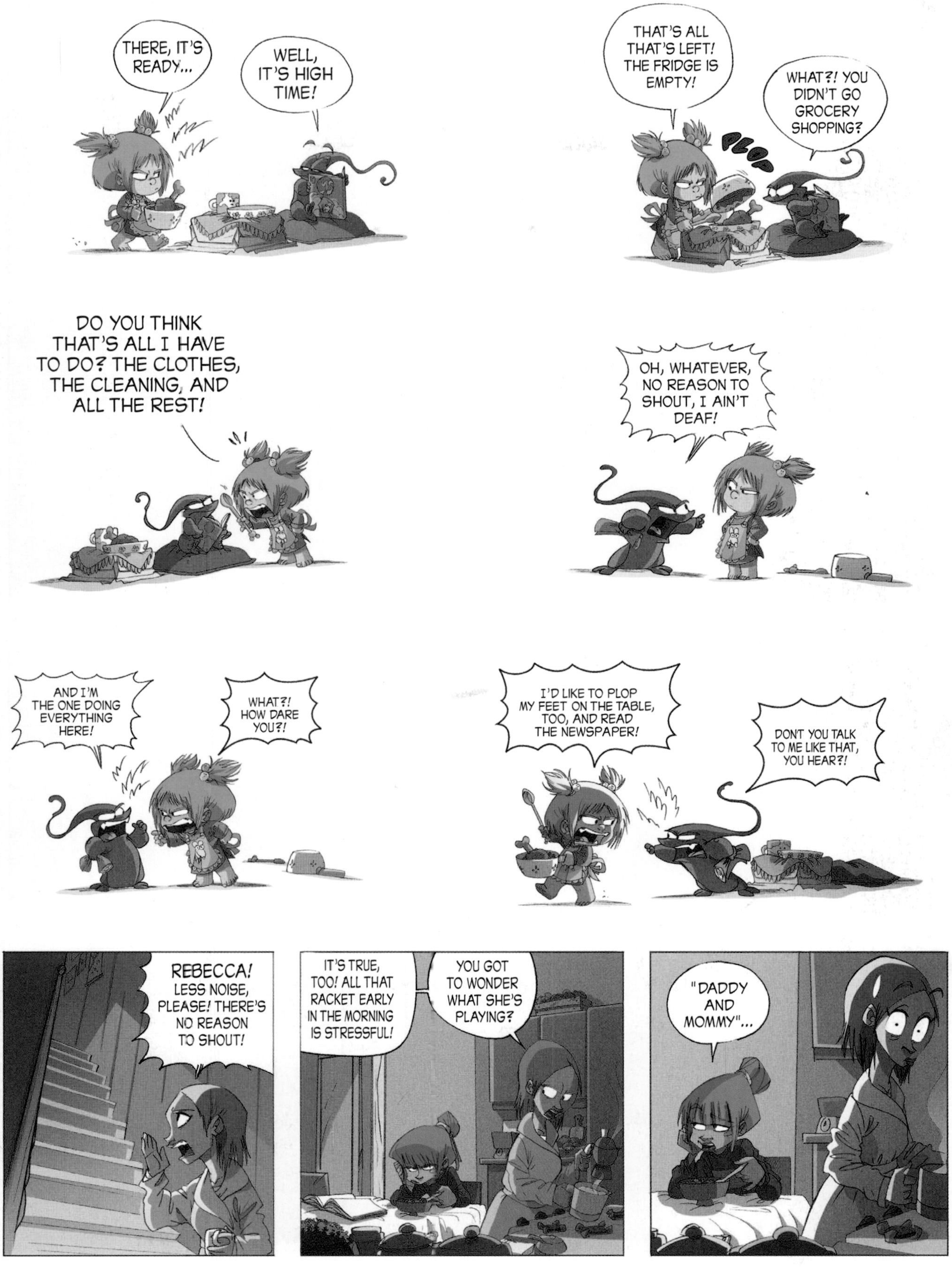
THERE, IT'S READY...
WELL, IT'S HIGH TIME!
THAT'S ALL THAT'S LEFT! THE FRIDGE IS EMPTY!
PLOP
WHAT?! YOU DIDN'T GO GROCERY SHOPPING?
DO YOU THINK THAT'S ALL I HAVE TO DO? THE CLOTHES, THE CLEANING, AND ALL THE REST!
OH, WHATEVER, NO REASON TO SHOUT, I AIN'T DEAF!
AND I'M THE ONE DOING EVERYTHING HERE!
WHAT?! HOW DARE YOU?!
I'D LIKE TO PLOP MY FEET ON THE TABLE, TOO, AND READ THE NEWSPAPER!
DON'T YOU TALK TO ME LIKE THAT, YOU HEAR?!
REBECCA! LESS NOISE, PLEASE! THERE'S NO REASON TO SHOUT!
IT'S TRUE, TOO! ALL THAT RACKET EARLY IN THE MORNING IS STRESSFUL!
YOU GOT TO WONDER WHAT SHE'S PLAYING?
"DADDY AND MOMMY"...

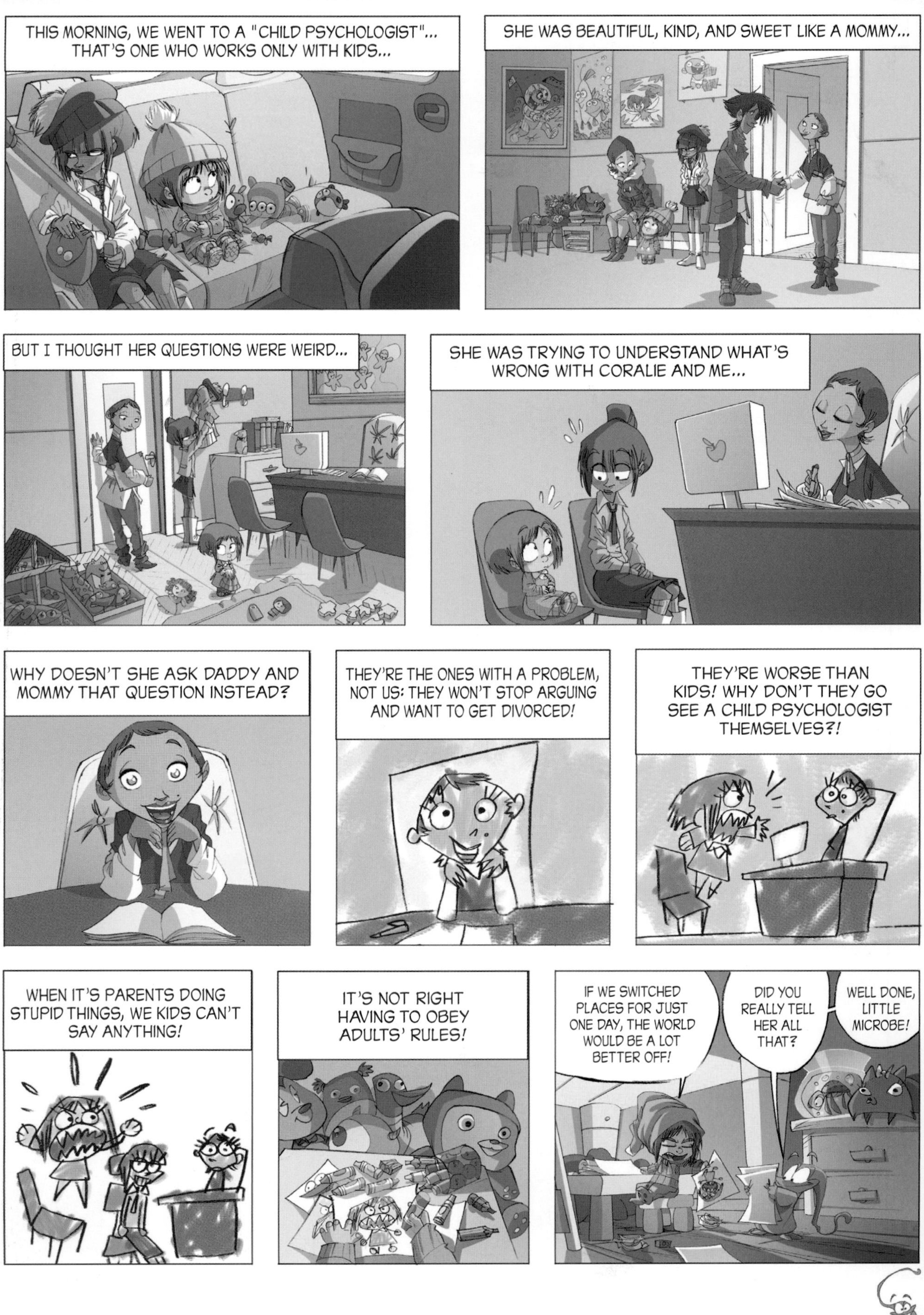
THIS MORNING, WE WENT TO A "CHILD PSYCHOLOGIST"... THAT'S ONE WHO WORKS ONLY WITH KIDS...
SHE WAS BEAUTIFUL, KIND, AND SWEET LIKE A MOMMY...
BUT I THOUGHT HER QUESTIONS WERE WEIRD...
SHE WAS TRYING TO UNDERSTAND WHAT'S WRONG WITH CORALIE AND ME...
WHY DOESN'T SHE ASK DADDY AND MOMMY THAT QUESTION INSTEAD?
THEY'RE THE ONES WITH A PROBLEM, NOT US: THEY WON'T STOP ARGUING AND WANT TO GET DIVORCED!
THEY'RE WORSE THAN KIDS! WHY DON'T THEY GO SEE A CHILD PSYCHOLOGIST THEMSELVES?!
WHEN IT'S PARENTS DOING STUPID THINGS, WE KIDS CAN'T SAY ANYTHING!
IT'S NOT RIGHT HAVING TO OBEY ADULTS' RULES!
IF WE SWITCHED PLACES FOR JUST ONE DAY, THE WORLD WOULD BE A LOT BETTER OFF!
DID YOU REALLY TELL HER ALL THAT?
WELL DONE, LITTLE MICROBE!

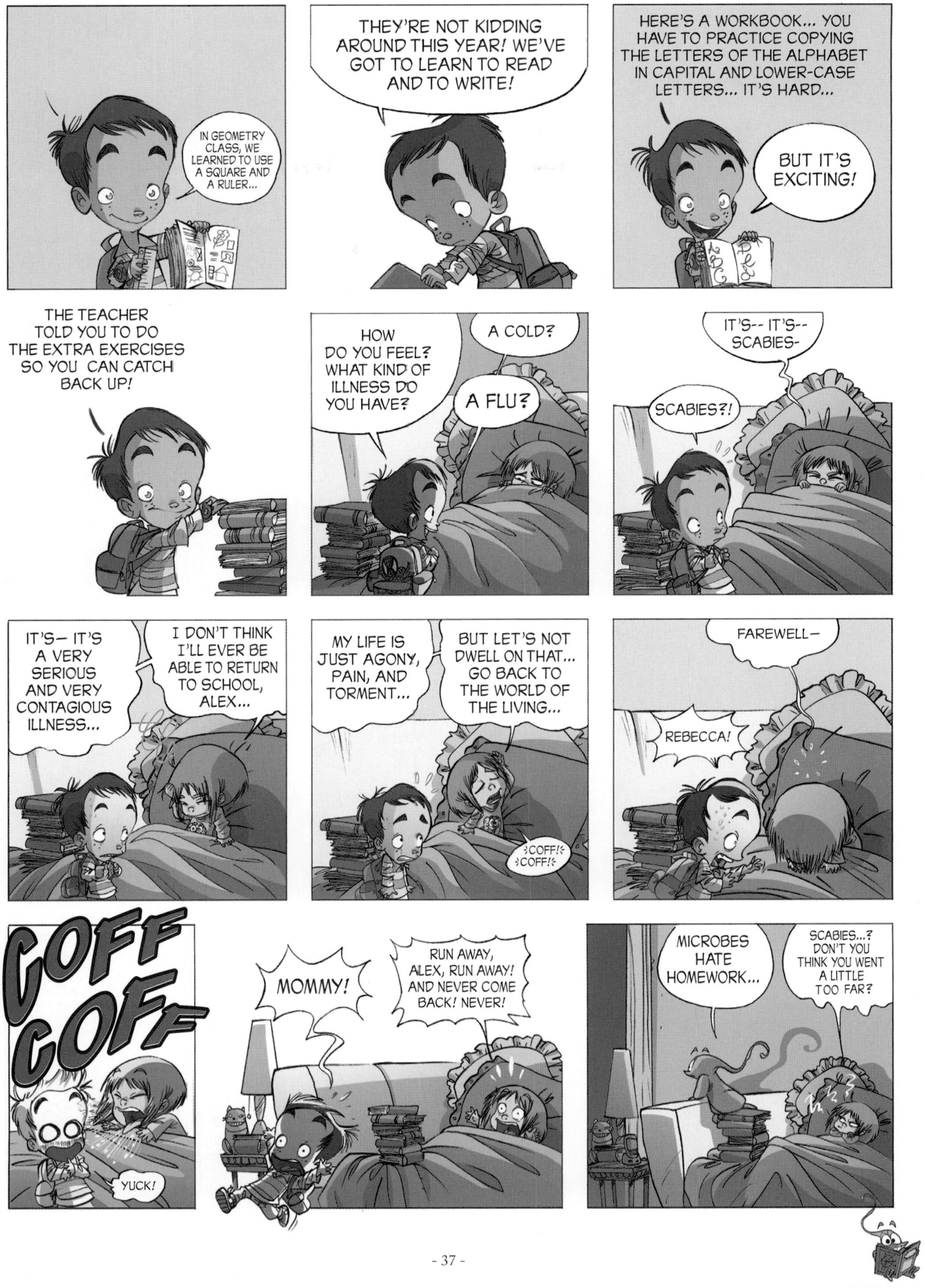
IN GEOMETRY CLASS, WE LEARNED TO USE A SQUARE AND A RULER...
THEY'RE NOT KIDDING AROUND THIS YEAR! WE'VE GOT TO LEARN TO READ AND TO WRITE!
HERE'S A WORKBOOK... YOU HAVE TO PRACTICE COPYING THE LETTERS OF THE ALPHABET IN CAPITAL AND LOWER-CASE LETTERS... IT'S HARD...
BUT IT'S EXCITING!
THE TEACHER TOLD YOU TO DO THE EXTRA EXERCISES SO YOU CAN CATCH BACK UP!
HOW DO YOU FEEL? WHAT KIND OF ILLNESS DO YOU HAVE?
A COLD?
A FLU?
IT'S-- IT'S-- SCABIES-
SCABIES?!
IT'S— IT'S A VERY SERIOUS AND VERY CONTAGIOUS ILLNESS...
I DON'T THINK I'LL EVER BE ABLE TO RETURN TO SCHOOL, ALEX...
MY LIFE IS JUST AGONY, PAIN, AND TORMENT...
BUT LET'S NOT DWELL ON THAT... GO BACK TO THE WORLD OF THE LIVING...
COFF! COFF!
FAREWELL—
REBECCA!
COFF COFF
YUCK!
MOMMY!
RUN AWAY, ALEX, RUN AWAY! AND NEVER COME BACK! NEVER!
MICROBES HATE HOMEWORK...
SCABIES...? DON'T YOU THINK YOU WENT A LITTLE TOO FAR?

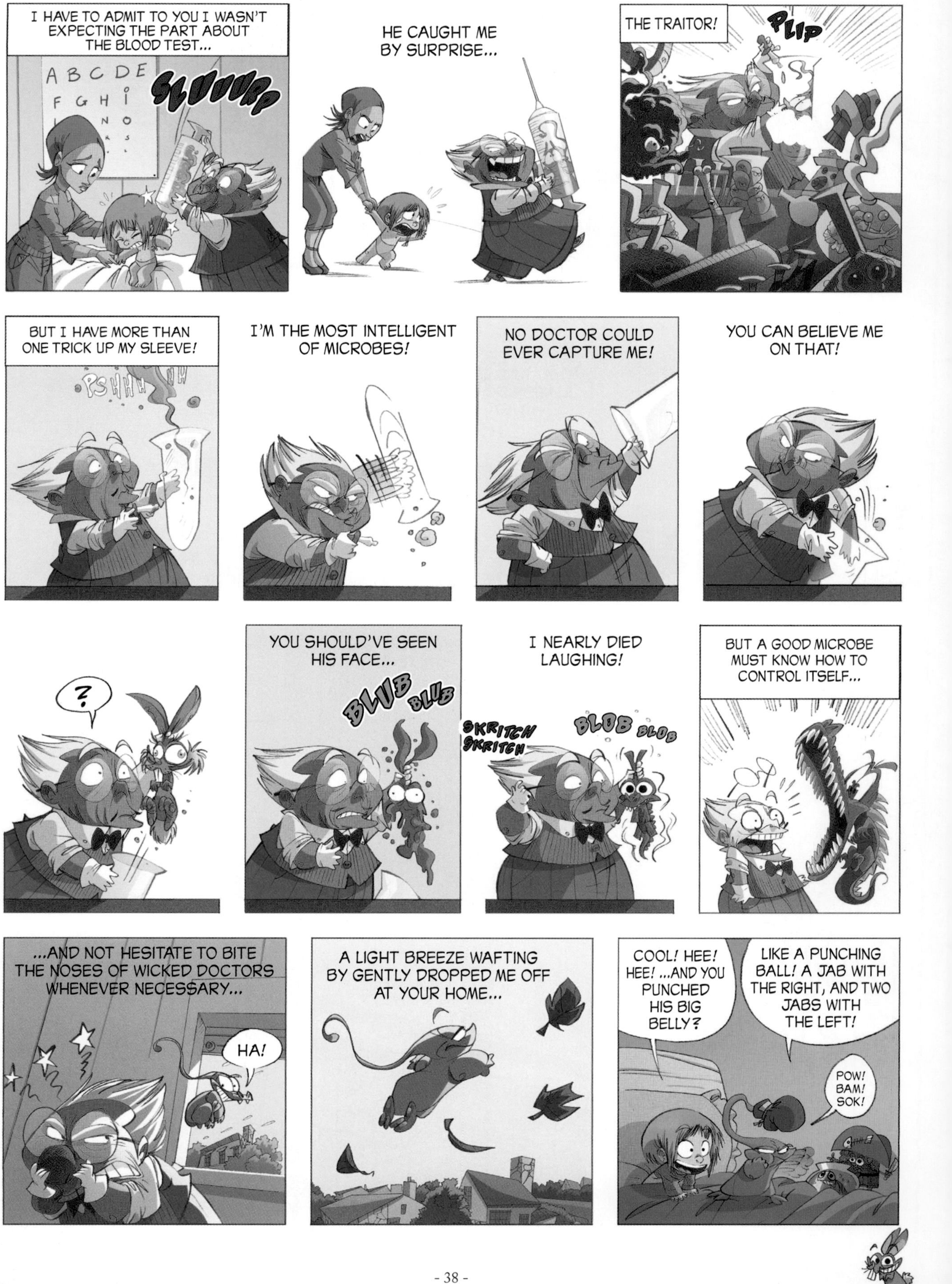
I HAVE TO ADMIT TO YOU I WASN'T EXPECTING THE PART ABOUT THE BLOOD TEST...
SLUUURP
HE CAUGHT ME BY SURPRISE...
THE TRAITOR!
PLIP
BUT I HAVE MORE THAN ONE TRICK UP MY SLEEVE!
I'M THE MOST INTELLIGENT OF MICROBES!
NO DOCTOR COULD EVER CAPTURE ME!
YOU CAN BELIEVE ME ON THAT!
?
YOU SHOULD'VE SEEN HIS FACE...
BLUB BLUB
I NEARLY DIED LAUGHING!
SKRITCH SKRITCH
BLOB BLOB
BUT A GOOD MICROBE MUST KNOW HOW TO CONTROL ITSELF...
...AND NOT HESITATE TO BITE THE NOSES OF WICKED DOCTORS WHENEVER NECESSARY...
HA!
A LIGHT BREEZE WAFTING BY GENTLY DROPPED ME OFF AT YOUR HOME...
COOL! HEE! HEE! ...AND YOU PUNCHED HIS BIG BELLY?
LIKE A PUNCHING BALL! A JAB WITH THE RIGHT, AND TWO JABS WITH THE LEFT!
POW! BAM! SOK!

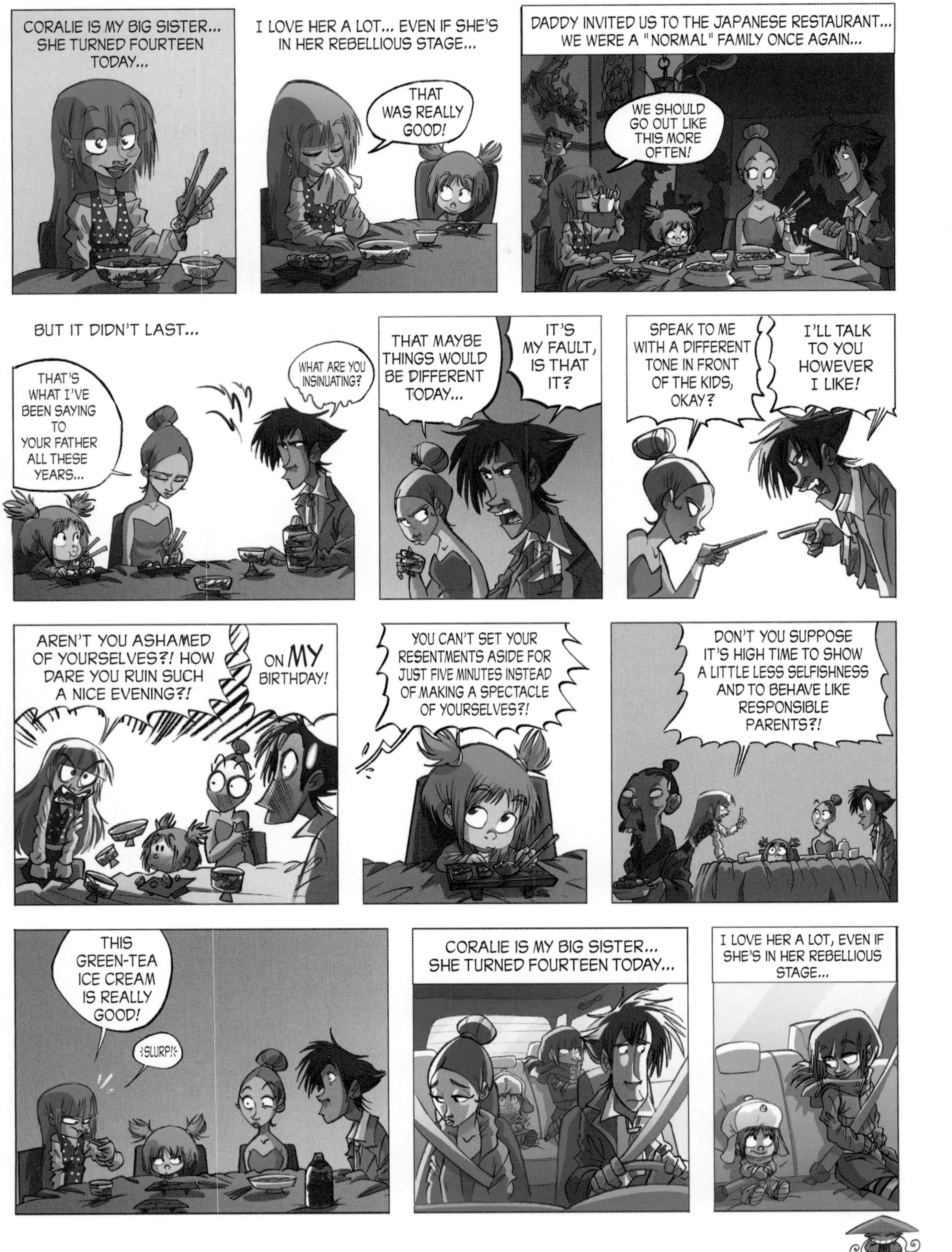
CORALIE IS MY BIG SISTER... SHE TURNED FOURTEEN TODAY...
I LOVE HER A LOT... EVEN IF SHE'S IN HER REBELLIOUS STAGE...
THAT WAS REALLY GOOD!
DADDY INVITED US TO THE JAPANESE RESTAURANT... WE WERE A "NORMAL" FAMILY ONCE AGAIN...
WE SHOULD GO OUT LIKE THIS MORE OFTEN!
BUT IT DIDN'T LAST...
THAT'S WHAT I'VE BEEN SAYING TO YOUR FATHER ALL THESE YEARS...
WHAT ARE YOU INSINUATING?
THAT MAYBE THINGS WOULD BE DIFFERENT TODAY...
IT'S MY FAULT, IS THAT IT?
SPEAK TO ME WITH A DIFFERENT TONE IN FRONT OF THE KIDS, OKAY?
I'LL TALK TO YOU HOWEVER I LIKE!
AREN'T YOU ASHAMED OF YOURSELVES?! HOW DARE YOU RUIN SUCH A NICE EVENING?!
ON MY BIRTHDAY!
YOU CAN'T SET YOUR RESENTMENTS ASIDE FOR JUST FIVE MINUTES INSTEAD OF MAKING A SPECTACLE OF YOURSELVES?!
DON'T YOU SUPPOSE IT'S HIGH TIME TO SHOW A LITTLE LESS SELFISHNESS AND TO BEHAVE LIKE RESPONSIBLE PARENTS?!
THIS GREEN-TEA ICE CREAM IS REALLY GOOD!
SLURP!
CORALIE IS MY BIG SISTER... SHE TURNED FOURTEEN TODAY...
I LOVE HER A LOT, EVEN IF SHE'S IN HER REBELLIOUS STAGE...

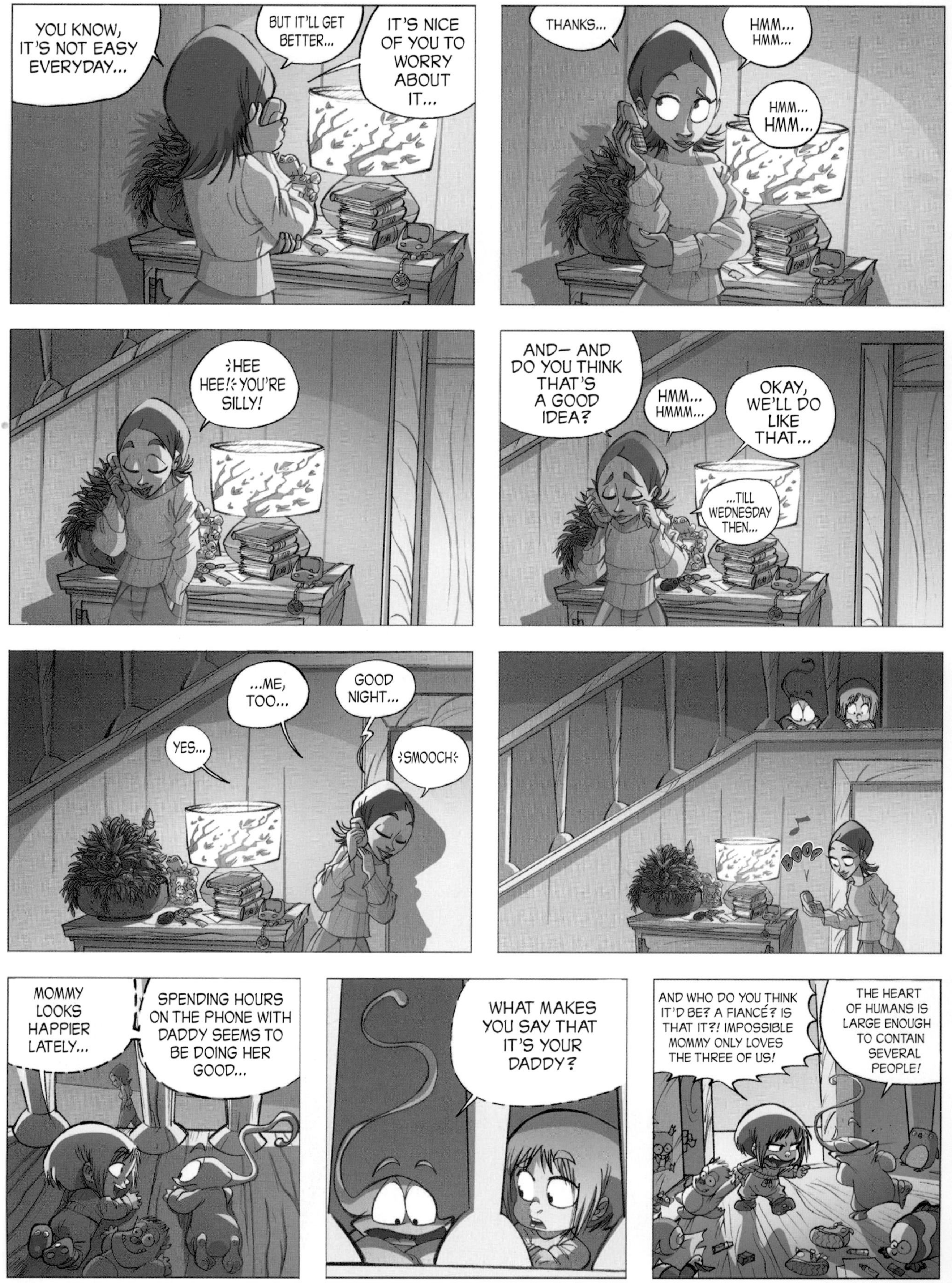
YOU KNOW, IT'S NOT EASY EVERYDAY...
BUT IT'LL GET BETTER...
IT'S NICE OF YOU TO WORRY ABOUT IT...
THANKS...
HMM... HMM...
HMM... HMM...
HEE HEE! YOU'RE SILLY!
AND— AND DO YOU THINK THAT'S A GOOD IDEA?
HMM... HMMM...
OKAY, WE'LL DO LIKE THAT...
...TILL WEDNESDAY THEN...
YES...
...ME, TOO...
GOOD NIGHT...
SMOOCH
BOOP
MOMMY LOOKS HAPPIER LATELY...
SPENDING HOURS ON THE PHONE WITH DADDY SEEMS TO BE DOING HER GOOD...
WHAT MAKES YOU SAY THAT IT'S YOUR DADDY?
AND WHO DO YOU THINK IT'D BE? A FIANCÉ? IS THAT IT?! IMPOSSIBLE MOMMY ONLY LOVES THE THREE OF US!
THE HEART OF HUMANS IS LARGE ENOUGH TO CONTAIN SEVERAL PEOPLE!

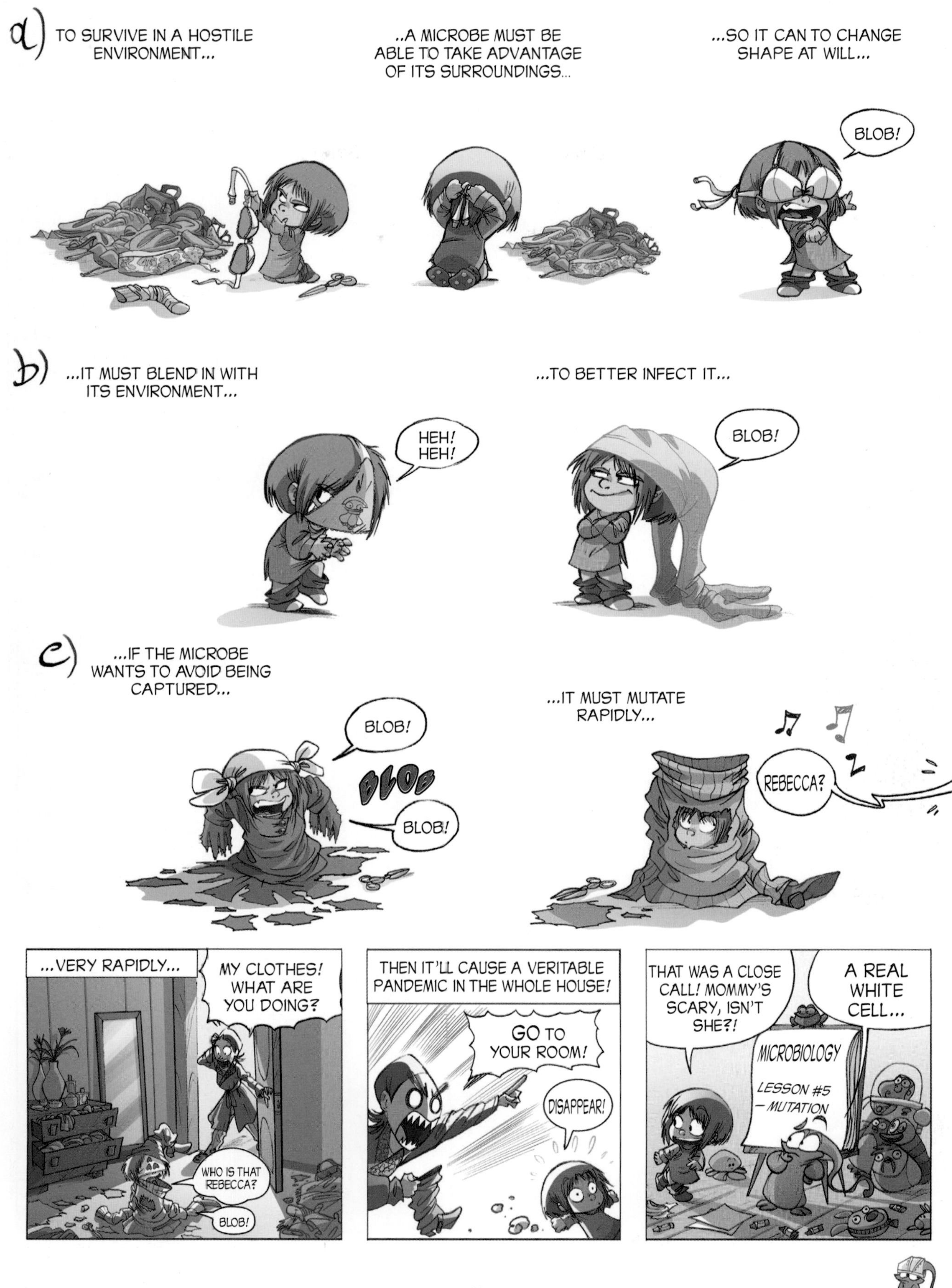
a)
TO SURVIVE IN A HOSTILE ENVIRONMENT...
..A MICROBE MUST BE ABLE TO TAKE ADVANTAGE OF ITS SURROUNDINGS...
...SO IT CAN TO CHANGE SHAPE AT WILL...
BLOB!
b)
...IT MUST BLEND IN WITH ITS ENVIRONMENT...
HEH! HEH!
...TO BETTER INFECT IT...
BLOB!
c)
...IF THE MICROBE WANTS TO AVOID BEING CAPTURED...
BLOB!
BLOB
BLOB!
...IT MUST MUTATE RAPIDLY...
REBECCA?
...VERY RAPIDLY...
MY CLOTHES! WHAT ARE YOU DOING?
WHO IS THAT REBECCA?
BLOB!
THEN IT'LL CAUSE A VERITABLE PANDEMIC IN THE WHOLE HOUSE!
GO TO YOUR ROOM!
DISAPPEAR!
THAT WAS A CLOSE CALL! MOMMY'S SCARY, ISN'T SHE?!
A REAL WHITE CELL...
MICROBIOLOGY
LESSON #5 – MUTATION

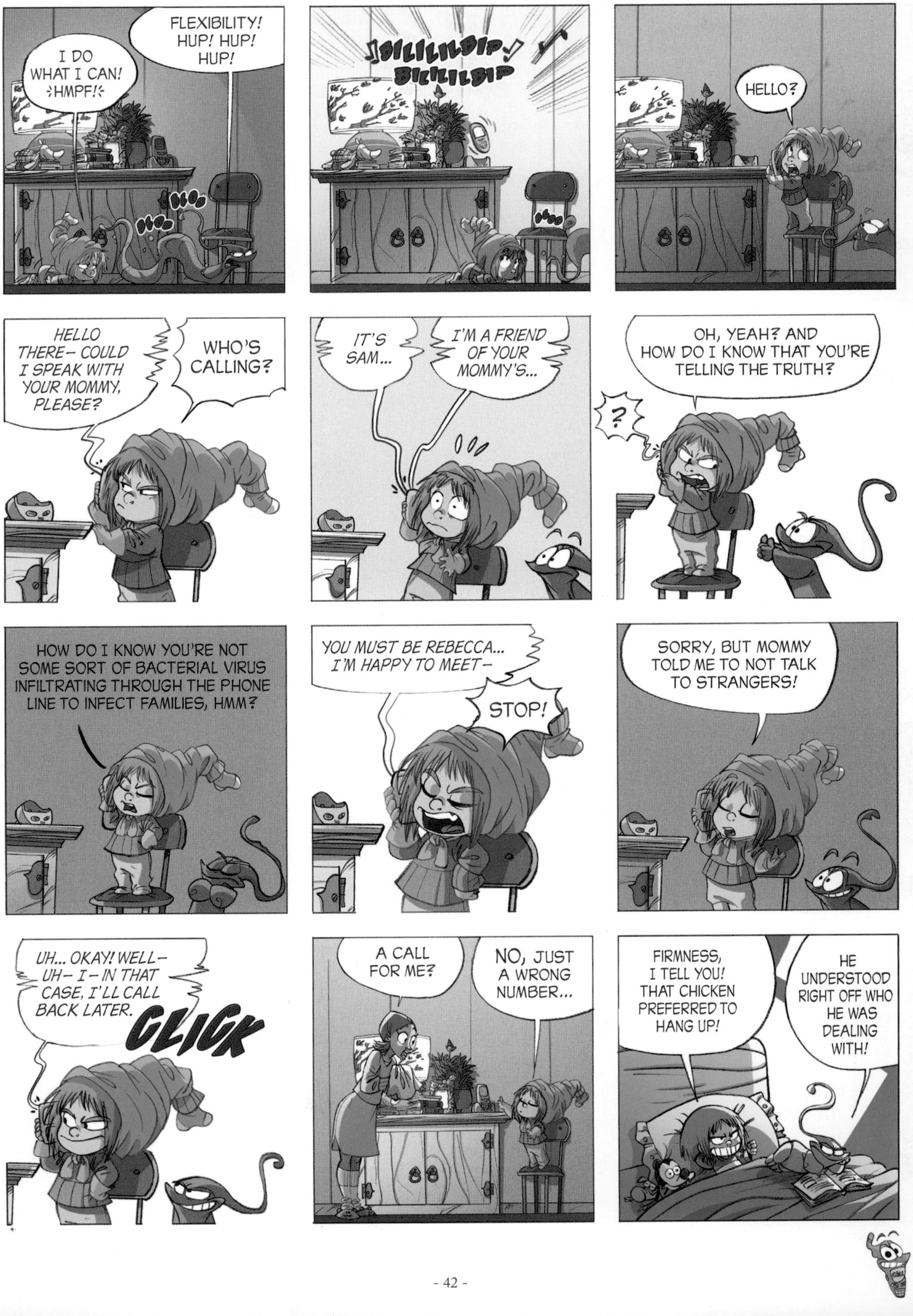
I DO WHAT I CAN! HMPF!
FLEXIBILITY! HUP! HUP! HUP!
BILILILBIP! BILILILBIP
HELLO?
HELLO THERE– COULD I SPEAK WITH YOUR MOMMY, PLEASE?
WHO'S CALLING?
IT'S SAM...
I'M A FRIEND OF YOUR MOMMY'S...
OH, YEAH? AND HOW DO I KNOW THAT YOU'RE TELLING THE TRUTH?
?
HOW DO I KNOW YOU'RE NOT SOME SORT OF BACTERIAL VIRUS INFILTRATING THROUGH THE PHONE LINE TO INFECT FAMILIES, HMM?
YOU MUST BE REBECCA... I'M HAPPY TO MEET–
STOP!
SORRY, BUT MOMMY TOLD ME TO NOT TALK TO STRANGERS!
UH... OKAY! WELL– UH– I– IN THAT CASE, I'LL CALL BACK LATER.
CLICK
A CALL FOR ME?
NO, JUST A WRONG NUMBER...
FIRMNESS, I TELL YOU! THAT CHICKEN PREFERRED TO HANG UP!
HE UNDERSTOOD RIGHT OFF WHO HE WAS DEALING WITH!

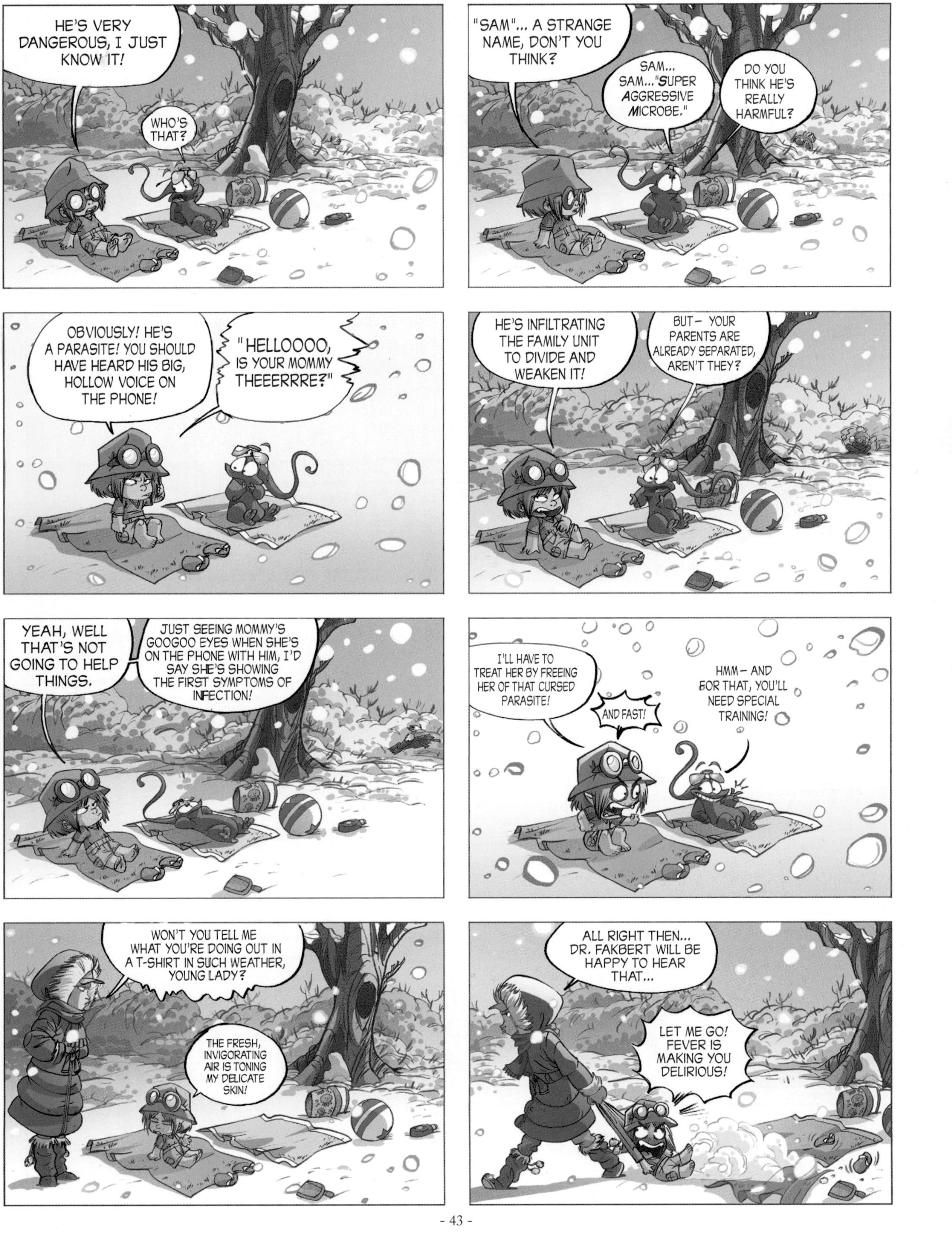
HE'S VERY DANGEROUS, I JUST KNOW IT!
WHO'S THAT?
"SAM"... A STRANGE NAME, DON'T YOU THINK?
SAM... SAM..."SUPER AGGRESSIVE MICROBE."
DO YOU THINK HE'S REALLY HARMFUL?
OBVIOUSLY! HE'S A PARASITE! YOU SHOULD HAVE HEARD HIS BIG, HOLLOW VOICE ON THE PHONE!
"HELLOOOO, IS YOUR MOMMY THEEERRRE?"
HE'S INFILTRATING THE FAMILY UNIT TO DIVIDE AND WEAKEN IT!
BUT– YOUR PARENTS ARE ALREADY SEPARATED, AREN'T THEY?
YEAH, WELL THAT'S NOT GOING TO HELP THINGS.
JUST SEEING MOMMY'S GOOGOO EYES WHEN SHE'S ON THE PHONE WITH HIM, I'D SAY SHE'S SHOWING THE FIRST SYMPTOMS OF INFECTION!
I'LL HAVE TO TREAT HER BY FREEING HER OF THAT CURSED PARASITE!
AND FAST!
HMM– AND FOR THAT, YOU'LL NEED SPECIAL TRAINING!
WON'T YOU TELL ME WHAT YOU'RE DOING OUT IN A T-SHIRT IN SUCH WEATHER, YOUNG LADY?
THE FRESH, INVIGORATING AIR IS TONING MY DELICATE SKIN!
ALL RIGHT THEN... DR. FAKBERT WILL BE HAPPY TO HEAR THAT...
LET ME GO! FEVER IS MAKING YOU DELIRIOUS!

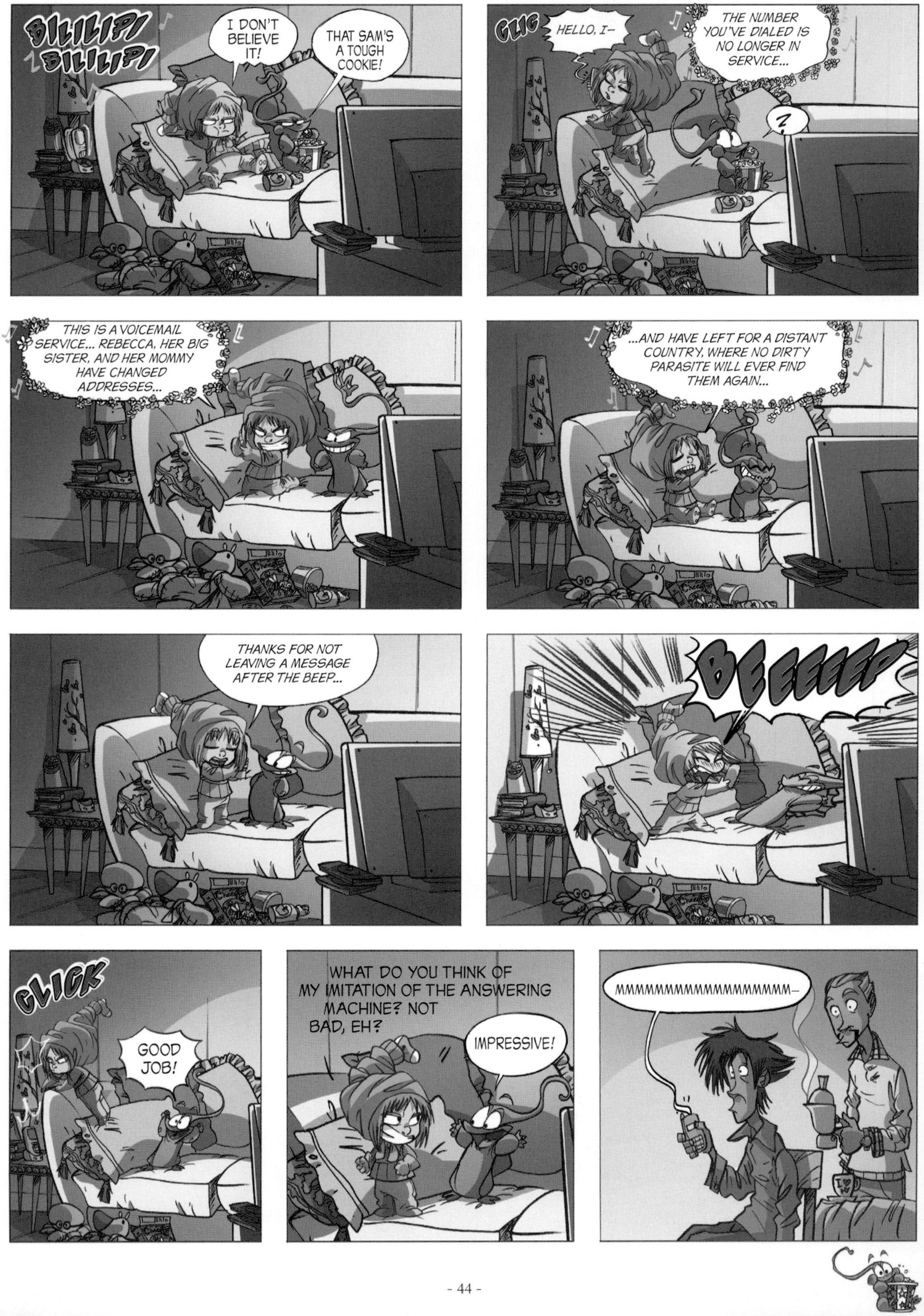
BILILIPI BILILIPI
I DON'T BELIEVE IT!
THAT SAM'S A TOUGH COOKIE!
CLIC
HELLO, I–
THE NUMBER YOU'VE DIALED IS NO LONGER IN SERVICE...
?
THIS IS A VOICEMAIL SERVICE... REBECCA, HER BIG SISTER, AND HER MOMMY HAVE CHANGED ADDRESSES...
...AND HAVE LEFT FOR A DISTANT COUNTRY, WHERE NO DIRTY PARASITE WILL EVER FIND THEM AGAIN...
THANKS FOR NOT LEAVING A MESSAGE AFTER THE BEEP...
BEEEEEP
CLICK
GOOD JOB!
WHAT DO YOU THINK OF MY IMITATION OF THE ANSWERING MACHINE? NOT BAD, EH?
IMPRESSIVE!
MMMMMMMMMMMMMMMMMM–

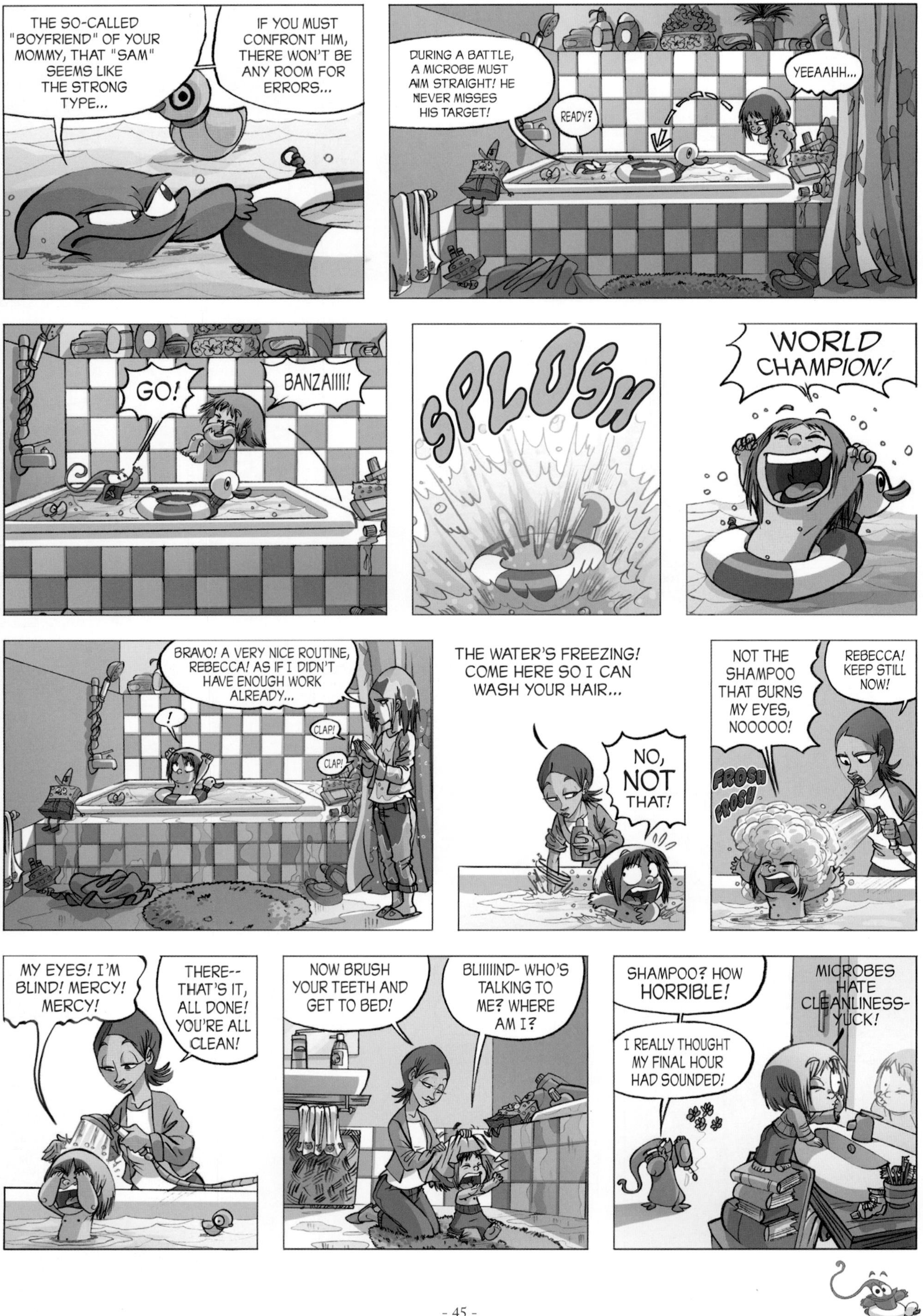
THE SO-CALLED "BOYFRIEND" OF YOUR MOMMY, THAT "SAM" SEEMS LIKE THE STRONG TYPE...
IF YOU MUST CONFRONT HIM, THERE WON'T BE ANY ROOM FOR ERRORS...
DURING A BATTLE, A MICROBE MUST AIM STRAIGHT! HE NEVER MISSES HIS TARGET!
READY?
YEEAAHH...
GO!
BANZAIIII!
SPLOSH
WORLD CHAMPION!
BRAVO! A VERY NICE ROUTINE, REBECCA! AS IF I DIDN'T HAVE ENOUGH WORK ALREADY...
!
CLAP!
CLAP!
THE WATER'S FREEZING! COME HERE SO I CAN WASH YOUR HAIR...
NO, NOT THAT!
NOT THE SHAMPOO THAT BURNS MY EYES, NOOOOO!
REBECCA! KEEP STILL NOW!
FROSH
FROSH
MY EYES! I'M BLIND! MERCY! MERCY!
THERE-- THAT'S IT, ALL DONE! YOU'RE ALL CLEAN!
NOW BRUSH YOUR TEETH AND GET TO BED!
BLIIIIIND- WHO'S TALKING TO ME? WHERE AM I?
SHAMPOO? HOW HORRIBLE!
I REALLY THOUGHT MY FINAL HOUR HAD SOUNDED!
MICROBES HATE CLEANLINESS- YUCK!

OF COURSE, YOUR PARENTS STILL LOVE YOU, REBECCA!
YOU'RE THEIR LITTLE GIRL!
!
...AND THEIR SEPARATION CHANGES NOTHING ABOUT THAT...
BUT WHY AREN'T THEY IN LOVE ANY LONGER THEN?
I DON'T KNOW WHY, REBECCA— THAT'S GROWN-UPS' BUSINESS!
AND THEN— YOUR PARENTS ARE GOING TO STAY GOOD FRIENDS, AREN'T THEY?
PLOOSH
YEAH... ADULTS ARE STILL DUMB...
IT'S LIKE THERE'S A HOLE IN MY HOME NOW...
A HOLE THAT'S LETTING IN DRAFTS OF AIR...
...AND DIRTY PARASITES!
IT'S REALLY STARTING TO GET ON MY NERVES! HE CALLS MOMMY EVERY DAY!
AS IF I DIDN'T ALREADY HAVE ENOUGH TO WORRY ABOUT!
MY GOODNESS! FROGS DON'T SEEM TO LIKE THE COLD VERY MUCH!
WHAT IF WE WENT AND DREW THEM A NICE WARM BATH?
THAT'S A GREAT IDEA, ERNEST!
DO YOU THINK MOMMY WILL AGREE?
YOU JUST DON'T HAVE TO ASK HER PERMISSION...
Bianco & Dalena

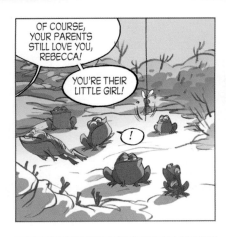

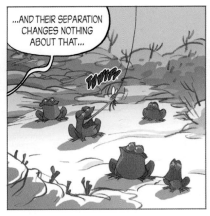

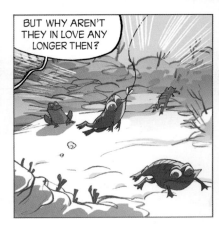

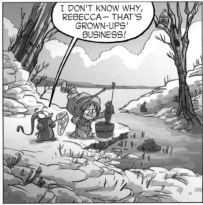

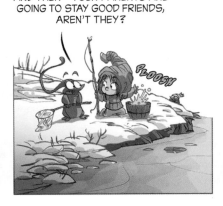

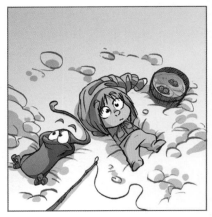

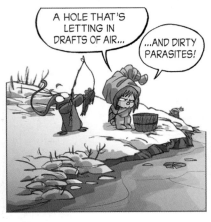

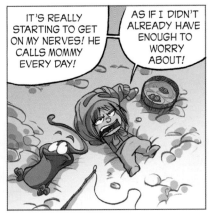

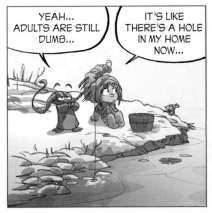

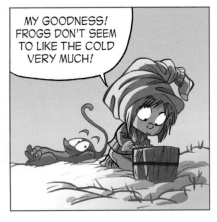

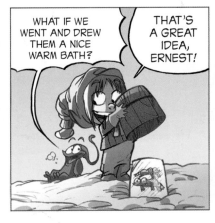

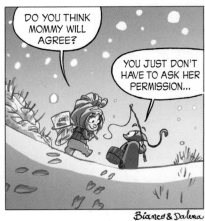

WATCH OUT FOR PAPERCUTZ™

Welcome to the first, sanitized-for-your-protection ERNEST & REBECCA graphic novel from Papercutz. By now you probably know who Ernest & Rebecca are, but you may not know what either a "graphic novel" or "Papercutz" are. Well, I'm Papercutz Editor-in-Chief Jim Salicrup, and I'm here to explain it all to you…

First, "graphic novel" is just a fancy-schmancy term for any kind of comics printed in book form. Secondly, "Papercutz" is the name, dreamed up by Sylvia Nantier, for the publishing company that was created by publisher Terry Nantier and me, and that is dedicated to publishing great graphic novels for all ages. Obviously, we believe that ERNEST & REBECCA is such a graphic novel, and that's why we're publishing it!

Written by Guillaume Bianco, and illustrated by Antonello Dalena, ERNEST & REBECCA truly is a wonderful graphic novel for all ages. Sensitively written, with believable human characters co-existing with fantastic yet virtually unseen microbes, all brought to stunning visual life by delightfully detailed graphics, that also are able to combine the common and ordinary with the wildly imaginative. Dalena's artwork perfectly complements Bianco's scripts, with highly expressive characters and creatures living in a very recognizable real world.

If you like ERNEST & REBECCA as much as we do, then you won't want to miss the next volume in the series: #2 "Sam the Repulsive." And if you can't wait until then, you may want to pick up another premiere Papercutz graphic novel series, available now at booksellers everywhere: SYBIL THE BACKPACK FAIRY #1 "Nina." Unlike Rebecca, the older Nina, is not making herself sick to deal with the problems in her personal life. Nina is simply trying to have as normal a life as possible when two magical creatures pop out of her backpack, the mysterious Pandigole and the fairy Sybil…

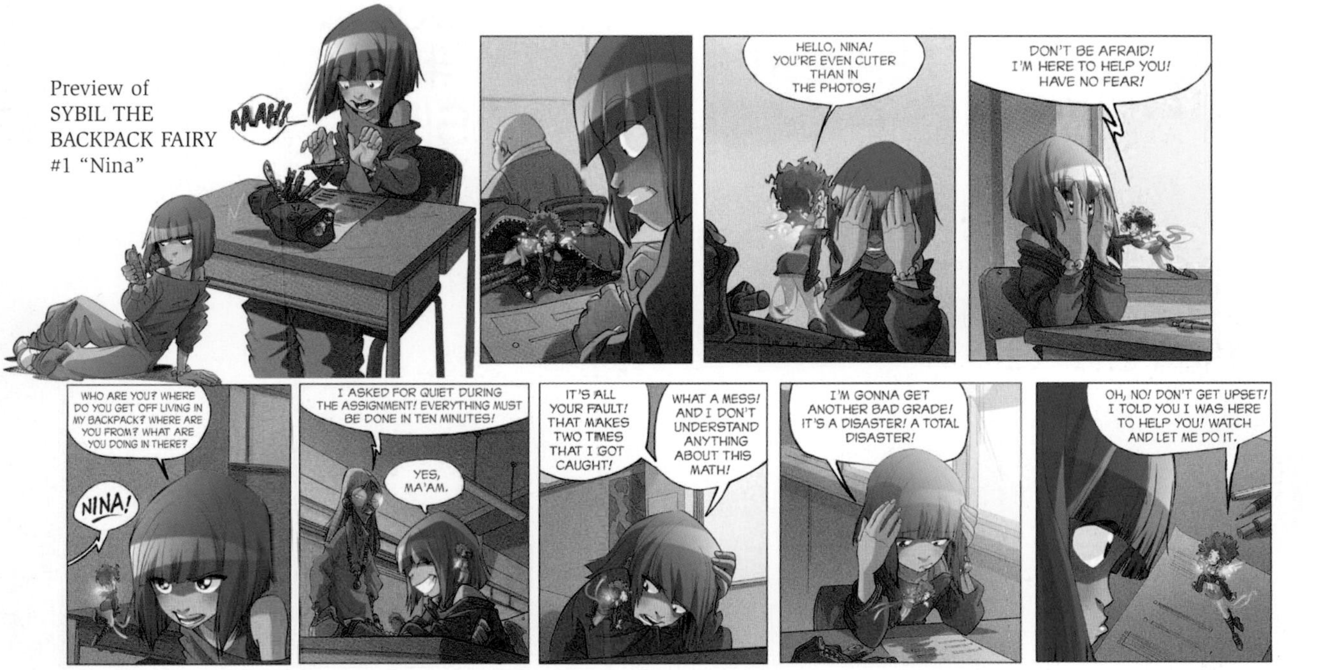
AAAH!
HELLO, NINA! YOU'RE EVEN CUTER THAN IN THE PHOTOS!
DON'T BE AFRAID! I'M HERE TO HELP YOU! HAVE NO FEAR!
WHO ARE YOU? WHERE DO YOU GET OFF LIVING IN MY BACKPACK? WHERE ARE YOU FROM? WHAT ARE YOU DOING IN THERE?
NINA!
I ASKED FOR QUIET DURING THE ASSIGNMENT! EVERYTHING MUST BE DONE IN TEN MINUTES!
YES, MA'AM.
IT'S ALL YOUR FAULT! THAT MAKES TWO TIMES THAT I GOT CAUGHT!
WHAT A MESS! AND I DON'T UNDERSTAND ANYTHING ABOUT THIS MATH!
I'M GONNA GET ANOTHER BAD GRADE! IT'S A DISASTER! A TOTAL DISASTER!
OH, NO! DON'T GET UPSET! I TOLD YOU I WAS HERE TO HELP YOU! WATCH AND LET ME DO IT.

Preview of SYBIL THE BACKPACK FAIRY #1 "Nina"

Let me, and everyone else at Papercutz, know what you think of ERNEST & REBECCA—you can email me at salicrup@papercutz.com or send an actual letter or post card to me at Papercutz, 40 Exchange Place, Suite 1380, New York, NY 10005. Whether you love or hate ERNEST & REBECCA, let us know! We really want to create the very best graphic novels we possibly can for you, so it really helps us when you let us know what you like or don't like. And be sure to go to www.papercutz.com for a peek at all the other great graphic novels, such as THE SMURFS, GERONIMO STILTON, DISNEY FAIRIES, and so many more, that we publish, as well as for all the latest news on ERNEST & REBECCA!

Thanks,

Jim

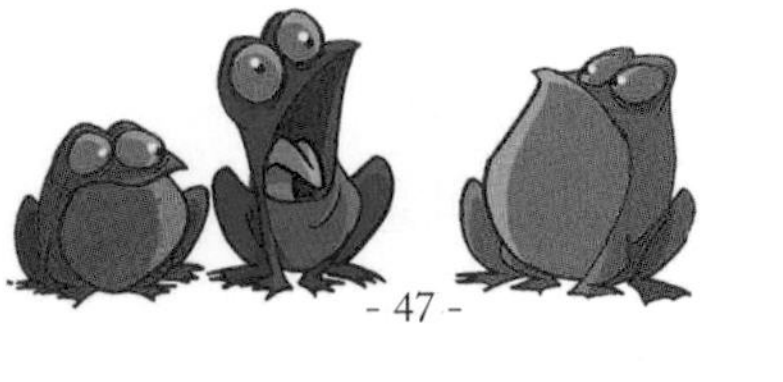

ERNEST AND REBECCA
WILL RETURN VERY SOON IN
ERNEST & REBECCA #2
"SAM THE REPULSIVE"